DARK EMBRACE

EVE SILVER

ALSO BY EVE SILVER

DARK GOTHIC SERIES

(Books in this series can be read in any order)

Dark Desires

His Dark Kiss

Dark Prince

His Wicked Sins

Seduced by a Stranger

Dark Embrace

THE SINS SERIES

Sins of the Heart (Book 1)

Sin's Daughter (Book 2, Novella)

Sins of the Soul (Book 3)

Sins of the Flesh (Book 4)

Body of Sin (Book 5)

NORTHERN WASTE SERIES

(Eve Silver writing as Eve Kenin)

Driven (Book 1)

Frozen (Book 1.5)

Hidden (Book 2)

~

Join Eve's Reader Group for the latest info about contests, new releases and more! www.EveSilver.net

www.evesilver.net

DARK EMBRACE

e-ISBN: 978-1-988674-13-1

print-ISBN: 978-1-988674-14-8

DEAR READER

Dark Embrace is a full length novel based on the novella "Kiss of the Vampire" originally released in the anthology Nature of the Beast. I have expanded the original novella to flesh out the characters, plot, setting, and conflicts. I loved this story when I wrote it as a novella, but the length constraint meant that I had to be spare and brief. I'm thrilled to bring this story to you in its fuller form.

I hope you enjoy DARK EMBRACE!

Eve

PROLOGUE

London, February 10, 1839

KILLIAN THAYNE COULDN'T SAY WHY HE NOTICED SARAH LOWELL—
there were night nurses and day nurses aplenty at King's College—but
notice her he did. It was an hour before dawn. She had come early for
her shift and she stood by the bed of a man who moaned against the
pain. She was not tall, but her posture made it seem as though she was.
And she was confident in her skill as she unwound the bandage from
the wound on his arm.

Killian stood in the corner, cloaked in darkness, and he watched
with interest as Miss Lowell lifted her candle, and examined the deep,
long slash that had been fixed with an adhesive plaster and tight
bandage.

The man on the bed groaned.

"Let me help you," she said softly.

The patient ceased his thrashing and stared at her. "How can you
help me? The surgeon said there's nothing more to be done. I'll heal or
I won't and it is out of his hands."

Miss Lowell looked around the room, wary. Once she appeared

certain that the other patients slept and no one else observed her, she said, "There *is* something to be done, and I would be pleased to do it. There is a piece of cloth in the wound and several small stones. I can remove them if you'll let me. And then I'll sew you up."

"You?" The man made a harsh laugh that turned into another groan.

"Me," she said. "After all, is not your wife a fine hand with a needle?"

The man stared at her, wary. "She is."

"I, too, am a fine hand with a needle. And I think sutures will do better for you than the plaster." She paused. "And it was not a surgeon but an apprentice who tended your wound, one with less than a year's experience. I have trained more than half my life. Do not let the fact that I am a woman sway you from accepting my care. I *can* help you."

He was silent for a long moment.

"I can help you if you'll let me," she said, her tone even, confident.

The patient hesitated a moment longer and then with a grimace, he offered a nod.

Miss Lowell hastened from his bed and when she returned, she stopped at the basin at the side of the ward and washed her hands. Then she drew close to the patient once more and set out red wine, pads, rolls of linen bandages, and a needle with waxed threads.

The first thing she did was give the patient some of the wine. A good portion of it.

"We must be as quiet as we can," she said. "Are you ready?"

Again, the patient offered a short nod.

She took a pad and rolled it into a cylinder. "Bite on this to stifle your pain."

He did as she instructed, but still, he groaned as she prodded in the wound with her small fingers. Killian was not surprised when she drew forth the cloth and stones she had described. He was not surprised when she washed the wound with red wine and dried it with the pads, then sewed it up with neat stitches and wrapped it tightly in linen bandages. And he was not surprised when she cautioned her patient to mention the care she had provided to no one. If anyone asked, he was to say that he could not recall who had stitched and dressed his wound.

Killian was not surprised because from the first second she had unwound the man's dressing she had portrayed confidence and experience. So, no, he was not surprised, but he *was* impressed.

She had the knowledge and hands of a surgeon. A trained surgeon. Somehow, this woman had studied medicine or apprenticed to a surgeon. Both options were impossible for no medical school would accept a woman, and no surgeon would take one on as an apprentice. But Killian did not doubt what he had seen.

Which made Miss Sarah Lowell very interesting, indeed.

❦ I ❦

London, November 3, 1839

DYING MOMENTS OF DARKNESS AND SHADOW FOUGHT TO STAVE OFF the first creeping fingers of the dawn as Sarah Lowell walked the familiar route through the edge of St. Giles, north of Seven Dials. Her boots rang on the wet cobbles as she ducked through the dim alleys and twisting lanes, past wretched houses and tenements, and rows of windows, patched and broken. Wariness was her sole companion.

A part of her was attuned to the street before her, the gloomy, faintly sinister doorways, the courtyards that broke from the thoroughfare. And a part of her was ever aware of the road behind, dim and draped in shadows and menace.

She was alone...or was she? The scrape of a boot sounded from somewhere behind her.

Would that it was the cold that made her shiver. But, no, it was unease that did the deed.

Her twice-daily trek along these streets and laneways was something other than routine. More times than not she felt as though unseen eyes watched her from the gloom, footsteps dogging her every move. In the months since her father's death, she had become increasingly aware that someone followed her.

Beneath her cloak, she closed her fist tighter around the handle of her cudgel. She never left her room in the lodging house in Coptic Street without the short, sturdy stick. With good reason.

St. Giles was not a place for a woman alone. But, unfortunately, poverty did not allow for over-particular standards. She had little choice in where she lived but she could—and did—choose to protect herself. She had neither the means, nor the inclination, to own a pistol, and she had considered—and discarded—the possibility of defending herself with a knife.

So, the cudgel it was, and she prayed she never found herself in a circumstance where she would be required to use it on another human being.

Should those prayers go unheeded, she suspected that surprise would be one thing in her favor. With her small frame, wide hazel eyes, and straight dark hair, she appeared young and delicate. She *was* young, but she was far from delicate. Any attacker would likely not expect the defense she would mount. Her father had always said she was sturdy in both body and spirit. She wished it had not taken his death and the desperate turn of her life to prove his assertions true.

She had spent years by her father's side, honing her muscles lifting and turning patients who could not do so for themselves, honing her mind under his tutelage, learning anatomy and surgery and the details of all manner of diseases. More recently, she had spent months under her landlady's watchful eye, pummeling a sack stuffed with old rags in order to learn how to wield the cudgel.

A muffled sound to her left made her spin and peer down the alley next to the darkened chandler's shop. Her heart gave a lurch in her breast, and she dragged her weapon free of her cloak.

With a loud belch, a man stumbled toward her then veered away to lean, panting, against the wall. Muttering and cursing with a drunken slur, he fumbled at the flap of his breeches. Then came the sound of a stream of liquid hitting the wall.

Turning away, Sarah walked on, skirting the refuse and detritus that littered the street. She slipped her weapon beneath her cloak once more and willed her racing pulse to settle.

The feeling of being watched, being stalked, oozed across her skin like a slug. She glanced back over her shoulder, but there was only the empty street and hollowed doorways behind her.

And the sounds of footsteps.

Swirling fog and mizzling rain settled on her like a shroud, clinging to her hair and skin and clothes, a cold, damp sheen. She quickened her pace and hurried on.

Her destination was Portugal Street and the old St. Clement Danes workhouse that now housed King's College Hospital where she worked as a day nurse. There was talk of a new building but a new building required funding and there was none to be had. So, for now, there were some hundred and twenty beds in the old workhouse, split into several overcrowded wards that offered care to the sick poor.

No one of wealth and means would step foot in King's College. By choice, the rich were cared for in their own homes, and because of it, they were more likely to survive. Her father had often been called on such visits, and Sarah had accompanied him to assist. But the poor could not afford such luxury—a doctor to attend their bedside, medicines to cure disease or ease their pain—and so they came to King's College, and often enough they died.

"They would die regardless," her father had pointed out many times when Sarah had bemoaned the plight of those without ample funds. "At least the hospital offers some hope, however small." He had been implacable in that belief.

Sarah had agreed with him then and still felt that way now. She worked every day among the sick poor and she could not bear to think that all her efforts were for naught, that there was no hope for them, or her.

"Hope matters," her father used to say, the words lifted by his smile. "There is power in belief." If she closed her eyes and concentrated very hard, she imagined she could hear his voice. She missed him. She missed their talks. She missed the way he saw her not only as a daughter but as a person, one with valid thoughts and opinions. She missed their lively debates, the smell of his tobacco, and even the way he slurped his soup. She missed his laugh. She missed their life.

Again, came the sound of footsteps behind her, the pace matched to her own. She stopped. They stopped. She walked on and they followed, neither speeding up nor slowing down and when she glanced back, there was only fog and darkness.

Almost there now. She strode past the crumbling graveyard, shoulders back, head high. It was a horrific irony that King's College Hospital was situated squarely between that graveyard and the slaughterhouses of Butcher's Row. She had her own well-guarded opinion that while some doctors and surgeons at King's College were dedicated souls bent on easing suffering, others might be better suited to work in the abattoirs.

At least there, death was an outcome both expected and sought after.

As the hospital loomed before her, she paused and glanced back once more. There, near the graveyard, she saw a black-cloaked figure clinging to the shadows, painted in shades of pewter and coal and ash. Watching. A shiver chased along her spine.

Each day, she walked to work in the predawn gloom and returned home after the sun had set. Many times, she had harbored unnerving suspicion that she was being followed, but proof of her supposition had, for the most part, been absent. This was only the second time that a form had actually materialized from the mist. Or had it? She stared hard at the spot, but could not be certain she saw anything more than a man-shaped shadow that could be cast by any one of the statues in the graveyard.

She had her cudgel in hand. She should walk to the gate and discover if it was statue or man that cast that shadow. And if it was a man? Her fingers tightened on her weapon.

She was torn between confronting the miscreant and avoiding such confrontation at all costs.

After a moment, she decided on the latter and headed for the doors of King's College. She hurried into the building and made her way first to the nurse's cloakroom, where she divested herself of her damp overgarment, then through the dim hallways to the women's sick ward. There was a patient here she wished to check on, a woman who was so ill she had not been able to eat or drink or even void for two days. It was as though her body refused to carry out the normal functions of life. Sarah hoped she had taken a turn for the better, though it was more likely that the woman had taken a turn for the worse.

She paused in the hallway near the ward. The first rays of dawn filtered through grimy windows to steal across the floor in pale slashes. The sounds of suffering carried through the place, eerie moans and louder cries, a sob, the creak of a bed as someone shifted, then shifted again.

Sarah stepped through the doorway and took a second to acclimate to the smell. No matter how much limewash was slapped on the plaster, no matter how many scrubbings with yellow soap the floors took, the smell—the metallic bite of blood, the raw-onion stink of old sweat, the harsh ammonia of urine—never quite melted away. These small battles might beat back the wretched stench for a time but, in truth, the war was long lost. The sick ward was forever infused with the vestiges of human misery.

Her gaze slid over the beds. Each one was full. Some even had two patients crowded into a space meant to hold only one.

In the corner was the bed she sought. Little light penetrated that far into the gloom. She took a step forward, then froze with a gasp.

There was someone sitting on a stool at the far side of the bed, a man, garbed all in black, the pale shape of the patient's partially upraised arm a stark contrast against the dark background offered by his coat.

He held the woman's wrist. Sarah could see that now. And she could see the breadth of his shoulders and the pale gold of his hair. She knew him then.

Killian Thayne.

Her pulse jolted at the realization. No matter how many times she saw him, how many times they interacted, she could not seem to put aside the schoolgirl infatuation that had struck her the first time they met. She rolled her eyes at her own foolishness.

She must have made a sound that alerted him to her presence, for he raised his head.

"Miss Lowell." His voice reached across the space that separated them, low, pleasant.

"Mr. Thayne," she acknowledged.

University-trained physicians were addressed as *doctor*, apprentice trained surgeons as *mister*, and there was a distinct barrier between them, not only at King's College but at any hospital throughout the city. Mr. Thayne belonged to the latter group.

"You are here early," he said, though he did not turn his head to look her way.

"As are you," she replied, unsurprised that he chose to engage her in conversation. On several previous occasions, there had been moments in the ward where Mr. Thayne walked his rounds and Sarah came to be in his path. To her befuddlement, and secret pleasure, he had deigned to speak with her, to ask her opinion of the patient's progress, to note her responses with interest and grave attention.

Once, he had even followed her suggestion, refusing to allow a patient with an open wound to be placed on a bed until the linens from the previous patient were removed and exchanged.

Matron had been aghast. "The linens already there will do," she had said. "The bed was made up fresh only a week ago, and the previous patient didn't soil them."

But Mr. Thayne was not to be swayed and thereafter he had insisted on clean linens each time a new patient entered the ward. The other surgeons scoffed, but Mr. Thayne remained resolute.

It was rare for a surgeon to consider the opinion of one of the nurses, even less so a day-nurse who was little more than a char. The fact that Mr. Thayne valued hers was a gift, one Sarah treasured. She had spent her life being treated as an intelligent being by her father. But at King's College, she was only a girl who served meals, cleaned bedpans, and changed soiled sheets, a fact that made an ugly slurry of resentment and anger and sadness mix in her gut. She had so much more to offer.

"It is not early for me," Mr. Thayne said, his tone holding a hint of dry amusement. He turned his head to look at her over his shoulder.

The thin light glinted off the spectacles Sarah had never seen him without, metal rimmed, the lenses a dark bottle-green. She wondered how he could see through them in the dimness.

"Late for you, then," she said, drifting closer. "You've been here all night?" He often was. Mr. Thayne seemed to prefer night to day.

"I have." He paused. "What brought you here a full half hour before the start of your shift?"

"My feet," Sarah said.

Mr. Thayne offered a soft huff of laughter. "Your skirt is wet."

Her cloak had not shielded her completely from the weather and the hem of her skirt was wet and dappled with mud. "The weather is inclement," she said.

Even in the dim light, she could see that he frowned. "I have not left the hospital for two nights and a day." He sounded as though that fact startled him, as though he had not, until this moment, marked the passage of time.

"It is not the first time," Sarah said, then pressed her lips together, realizing her words made clear that she was aware of his comings and goings and wishing she could call them back.

"No, it is not," he said.

"It was kind of you," she blurted. "To give Mrs. Carmichael the coats." Mrs. Carmichael was the night watch nurse in the surgical ward. Mr. Thayne had given her warm coats for her two growing sons.

"I am not kind," Mr. Thayne replied. "I was merely disposing of items which no longer appealed to me."

"Of course," Sarah replied. "The fact that they had clearly never been worn and were both far too small to have ever..." She broke off, unwilling to state aloud that the coats were sized for adolescents and would never have fit Mr. Thayne's broad-shouldered form, for that would be a clear admission that she *noticed* his broad-shouldered form. "Those coats will be put to good use."

"That is my hope," he said before turning his attention back to the patient.

She meant to walk away then, but something held her in place and she stood frozen, staring at the patient's white forearm where it contrasted with the cloth of Mr. Thayne's black-clad form.

A moan sounded from behind her, drawing her attention. "Water," came a woman's plea. "I am so thirsty. Please, water."

The night watch nurse was curled in the far corner of the sick ward by the fire, sleeping. Sarah could not help but feel pity for her, a widow with three small children who, after working the day as a charwoman came to sit the night through for a shilling and her supper, leaving her little ones with a neighbor, and paying her in turn.

She had not the heart to deny the woman a few stolen moments of rest, so she turned away to tend to the patient herself.

When she was done, she looked back to where she had seen Mr. Thayne.

He was gone, the patient asleep, her head lolled to one side, her arm hanging across the far edge of the bed.

Another patient called out. Sarah hesitated, wariness prickling through her. Stepping forward, she almost went to the patient Mr. Thayne had been tending. Then she wondered what she was thinking. What could she do for her that he had not? The woman was sleeping now. Best to leave her undisturbed.

Again, a voice behind her called out, becoming more insistent. Sarah helped the woman sit up and take a drink of water. When she was done, she noted the time and then made her way to the surgical ward.

Only hours later did she learn that the patient Killian Thayne had tended had died in the silvered moments when night turned to day, discovered by the night nurse when she roused from her slumber.

Only then did Sarah hear the whispers that the woman's wrist had been torn open, with nary a drop of blood spilled to mark the sheets.

Mr. Simon, the head surgeon, determined that the patient had injured herself on a sharp edge of the bedstead, and in truth, they found a smear of blood there that offered some proof of the supposition. But there were no bloodstains on the sheets or the floor. No blood congealed in the wound. And the woman herself looked like a dry husk, as though something had drained her of both blood and life.

Death was no stranger to King's College. But this manner of death would be strange anywhere, all the more so because it had happened before. Two months ago, a man had died in the surgical ward with his wrist torn open and no blood to be found. Three weeks after that, it had been a woman, dead in her bed, a dried-out husk.

And now, a third person, dead in a manner both strange and frightening.

Throughout that day and well into the night, Sarah could not dispel the memory of Killian Thayne, swathed in darkness, his head bowed, and the woman's arm white against the black of his coat.

Bergen, Norway, 1349

KJELL MISSED THEM: HIS PARENTS, HIS THREE LITTLE SISTERS, HIS BABY *brother. Not so little anymore. He'd been gone for three years. The baby would be walking. The oldest of his sisters might be married. His mother would say it was long past time that he married. Maybe she would be right. There was a farm a day's travel from theirs with four pretty daughters. At least, there had been four of them when he'd left. If there was even one yet unmarried, he might offer for her.*

He'd left his parents' farm to find his own way. He'd signed on with a merchant ship carrying dried fish. That time, they brought back salt from Lübeck. Other times it was cloth or spices. They sailed to ports far from the life he'd known in more than just distance; they were worlds away in sights and sounds and smells, each place foreign and fascinating. Oh, he'd been back to Bergen many a time over the years, but there had never been a chance to go home because it was an overland trek and because...well, because he'd always felt like tomorrow would be a good day to go, or the tomorrow after that.

But on this most recent trip he hadn't just seen wonders, he'd seen the effects of the Black Death. His shipmates had lost friends and family. Men he met in other ports spoke of the sweeping plague that decimated families, towns, cities. So, Kjell decided he would not wait for the tomorrow after tomorrow to go home. Today was the day.

With a grin, he glanced around the harbor. There was an English ship newly arrived, carrying a cargo of cloth. The men from that ship bumped shoulders with the men from his as they all moved away from the docks. He found himself in the midst of a group of them as they shouldered past. They were like a tide, and he rode it until he cleared the crowd. One of the men from the English ship fell into step beside him. He was pale with dark rings beneath his eyes, his brow dotted with sweat. He tripped and fell against Kjell, mumbling an apology as he coughed into his hand. Kjell helped the man right himself then stepped away and moved on, heading for home.

"Kjell!" His mother cried as he walked through the door. She threw her arms around him, laughing and crying and he was not ashamed to feel the prick of tears in his own eyes as he looked at his brother and his sisters. He threw his arms around each of them in turn. His father clapped him on the back, and Kjell clapped him in return.

"You've grown wider," his father said with a laugh, pressing his palms against the sides of Kjell's shoulders.

"As have you, but in a different direction," Kjell said, tapping his father's round belly. His father cuffed the side of his head in good-natured play and they both laughed.

When the evening meal was eaten, tales of Kjell's travels told while he dandled his brother on his knee and teased his sisters mercilessly, his father sent his siblings off to bed.

"Is it true what we hear?" his father asked once they were alone. "The Black Death? Is it truly so bad? They say it kills everyone, a terrible death. That it cuts entire families down within days."

"I haven't seen it myself," Kjell said. "I've only heard it's a terrible thing. They say it can go into the chest and starve a man of his breath. It can make tumors in the armpit or the groin, and then—" He broke off as his mother joined them.

She took his hands in hers and held them, her face lit with joy. "I am so glad to have you home."

He was glad to be home. He'd been lonely these last months, for the thrill of adventure had faded after years on a ship and in unfamiliar ports. As his mother spoke of the crops and the neighbors, he was lulled into relaxation. His eyes began to feel heavy and slid shut for but a moment. He was tired beyond tired, more exhausted than he could ever recall.

His mother rested her palm against his cheek. "Rest, Kjell. Tomorrow is another day."

He woke in the morning to find his head pounding and his skin clammy, his body trembling, hot one instant, cold the next. By that night, he had black swellings the size of apples in his armpits. Pain clawing at his insides, and he was so weak he could not stand.

Two of his three sisters and his brother fell ill the next morning.

His third sister and his mother took sick that night.

His father, who became ill last, died first.

The others followed within hours. They all died, save his mother who lay insensate, unmoving. Only the fluttering of her chest told Kjell she yet lived. He had heard tales that some survived. She could survive. He needed to believe it. The possibility that his mother might live was the tether that held his spirit to his body, the incentive he needed to keep fighting his own fight against the agony that consumed him.

He was sick in body, in mind, in spirit. Sick at heart. He had done this vile deed; he had brought this disease to them. He knew what it was. Plague. The Black Death. He knew it was the man from the English ship, the one with the cough who had visited this death upon him.

And he upon them, his precious family, all those he loved.

He had killed them all.

He lay shaking in his childhood home, surrounded by their bodies and he was too sick and weak to even tend to their corpses. He closed his eyes, despair and horror at what he had done moving sluggishly like an ichor in his veins.

The door burst open, letting in a blast of frigid air. A man filled the doorway, and beyond him, Kjell saw the stars of the night sky. He tried to rise, to warn him away from this place of death, but he was weak, so weak. And then he saw the man's face, his lips drawn back to bare his teeth, his eyes crazed.

"Is not one alive?" the man cried. He sounded desperate, agonized.

Kjell's mother moaned then, a sound that was little more than a breath.

The stranger lurched forward and fell upon her, tearing at her throat with his teeth. Kjell tried to rise only to find himself writhing on the floor as the pains in his gut sawed at him. Horrific sounds filled his ears, gurgling, gasping

—these from his mother. And the sounds of the stranger feeding, greedy and vile.

It was no man that had come here this night, but a monster.

Or was there no man at all, only a thing conjured by Kjell's fevered nightmares? Was he in truth alone here with only the dead for company? He could not separate truth from falsity.

Blackness shaded the edges of his vision, then the whole of it. His lids were weighted and he could not fight the darkness.

When he opened his eyes, the monster had become a man once more.

He sat by Kjell's side and stared at him with sunken eyes, sad and full of regret.

"You are dying," the stranger said.

He didn't want to die.

"Are you certain?" the man asked, and only then did Kjell realize he had spoken the words aloud. "There are worse things than death."

Kjell's eyes closed, but he forced them open once more. And he saw his mother's body. She was dead, her throat opened, but very little blood to mark the wound.

"You see?" the stranger said. "Things worse than death. I did not wish to do that. But I could not help myself." He buried his face in his hands. "The farms in this land are days' journey from each other. I stopped at three before I stumbled on this one." He lifted his head and looked at Kjell once more. "They were dead. All of them. At every farm I passed, they were dead. The plague. And with each farm, my hunger grew until it became a living thing unto itself." He paused. "I needed one alive. The hunger..."

"What are you?" Kjell asked.

"I am a creature of evil." There were loathing and despair in his tone.

"I will kill you for what you have done here." A fruitless vow. Kjell could barely summon the strength to speak, his words slow and slurred.

"Would that you could," the stranger said with a bitter laugh. "But you cannot." He looked away, then back toward Kjell. "You are so quick to pass judgment against me. I wonder what you would do in my place. You say you do not want to die. Well, I will give you that in payment for what I stole. A life for a life." His tone was dark and ugly and made the hairs at Kjell's nape rise. "You will see," the man said. "You will see."

He caught Kjell's hand in an iron grip, and though he struggled, he was too weak and the stranger too strong. The man lowered his head and a sharp pain sank deep into Kjell's wrist.

Bile crawled up the back of Kjell's throat. He struggled and tried to jerk away, the sensation of teeth gnawing at him and the sucking pull of the man's mouth made his stomach churn and his thoughts howl. He grew weaker and weaker, dark spots dancing before his eyes, and finally, he drifted away.

Drink.

Kjell's mouth tasted like copper and ash. Like blood.

Swallow. *An order.*

Too weak to move, to protest, he swallowed. Again and again.

He knew not how long he lay there, insensate. When he opened his eyes, the man stood in the open doorway, the first rays of the sun touching the horizon, turning it from black to gray.

"Watch it rise," the stranger said. "Watch as though it is your last sunrise." He made a choked sound that might have been a laugh or a sob. "Because it is."

Through the open door, Kjell watched the dawn until the bright ball of the sun was surrounded by a sky of uninterrupted blue. And then the man, this nameless man, this monster stepped through the doorway and stood in the light, arms outstretched to his sides. As Kjell watched, the stranger crumbled to ash, his clothes falling in a loose pile to mark the place he had last stood.

3

Weeks passed and the whispers about the strange deaths at King's College waned.

As was her habit, Sarah crept through her lodging house long before dawn, taking care to avoid the creaking stair and the floorboard in the corridor that groaned under the slightest weight. The building was old, musty, her chamber small and dark and damp, but it was inexpensive and the landlady was kind, both high recommendations as far as Sarah was concerned.

She had seen Mr. Thayne several times in the wards in recent days; there was nothing unusual in that.

She had dreamed of him last night; there was nothing unusual in that either. In her dream, he had stood between her and the shadowy form that followed her through the alleys of St. Giles. An interesting thing, given that she had not been plagued by the man who watched her in over a week. She almost dared hope that she had imagined the whole of it, that there was no man, no shadow, no threat.

As she passed the open door to the dining room, her landlady's voice carried from the darkness, slurred words and a petulant tone. "Rent's due. And why're you leaving so early?"

Sarah turned and lifted her candle to find Mrs. Cowden sitting on a chair in the dining room, elbows on the table, palms cupping her chin. There was an empty bottle of gin lying on its side on the floor.

"Have you been here all night?" Sarah asked as she retrieved the empty bottle and set it upright on the table.

"I have," Mrs. Cowden said. "My bed seemed too far away. Too quiet." She paused. "Mr. Cowden's been gone a year today. Or was it yesterday?" She paused again. "He used to make me laugh. We'd laugh and talk and sometimes he'd hum a tune and grab me about the waist and dance me around the parlor." She looked around as though expecting Mr. Cowden to step from the shadows at any second. Then she closed her eyes, lowered her forearms to the tabletop, and fell forward to rest her forehead on her crossed wrists. Just when Sarah thought she was asleep, she sat up straight and pinned Sarah with a sorrowful gaze. "It's a heartsick thing, missing someone you love."

"Come along, now," Sarah said holding out her hand. "I'll help you to bed. But we must be quick. I can't be late."

Mrs. Cowden ignored the offer of her hand. Instead, she patted the chair beside her. "Sit," she said. "Talk to me. Talk to me for just a little while. I am lonely."

A heaviness settled in the center of Sarah's chest, the weight challenging her every breath. But she refused to succumb to melancholy. "How can you be lonely when your house is full of people?" she asked with a forced smile.

"They're gone all day, working for the coin to pay the rent. And they sleep all night. And even when they are about, they are not him. I feel as if my arm is missing. My right arm." Mrs. Cowden sighed. "I miss him so."

Sarah swallowed against the lump in her throat. "I know."

Peering up at her with a poorly focused gaze, Mrs. Cowden said, "Rent's due."

Sarah patted her hand. "I paid the rent three days ago."

Mrs. Cowden narrowed her eyes. "You wouldn't lie to an old lady, would you?" She frowned and lifted a finger. "No...wait...you *did* pay the rent. I remember now. You are a good girl. Smart, too." She stared up at Sarah, her brown eyes unfocused. Seconds ticked past then Mrs.

Cowden asked, "What do you want, my dear? Truly want? Surely it is more than what you have. You should have more, a girl like you..."

Sarah hesitated, then said, "I want many things."

"A handsome husband. Children. All women want that," Mrs. Cowden said with a nod, and Sarah made no effort to correct her. It wasn't that she *didn't* want a husband and children. It was that she wanted many other things as well, most of which she would likely never have.

"I wanted children," Mrs. Cowden said. "I had three, you know."

"I know," Sarah said, and rubbed the woman's shoulder.

"They all died. Babes so small, dressed in white, sleeping in tiny coffins. I wanted more, but they never came. Mr. Cowden said we had each other and we were blessed to have that. He said that wanting more would only make me cry." Tears welled and spilled over Mrs. Cowden's lower lashes to wet her wrinkled cheeks. "He's dead," she said. "Dead and buried." She caught Sarah's hand, squeezing hard, her gaze intent. "Tell me, my dear. Tell me one thing you want with all your heart. I know it is something grand." She nodded. "I know."

Sarah said nothing.

"Tell me," Mrs. Cowden whispered, the words thick and slow. Then her gaze grew unfocused once more, her grip loosened, and she slumped forward, her cheek pressed to the table.

"What do I truly want?" Sarah said as Mrs. Cowden emitted a soft snore. "I want to ease the suffering of others. I want to *learn*, to become a vessel of great knowledge, to satisfy the curiosity that burns inside me." She bent and retrieved Mrs. Cowden's shawl from the floor. "I want friendships that feed my mind and soul with lively discourse and debate. I want to be a surgeon." She set the shawl around the woman's shoulders and stroked her back. "I want to have a great and terrible love, one that is worth any price."

They were dreams. Only dreams. But dreams were the food of the soul and Sarah refused to stop dreaming, no matter how unlikely her success and how meager her circumstance. "I want a life well lived," she whispered. "One that matters."

But another soft snore told her only the shadows were listening.

She snuffed the candle and left the room, left the house, and began her walk to King's College.

The grim weather of the past week had eased, leaving the temperature cold and crisp. No rain. No clouds. Only the dark predawn sky. And the sound of footsteps behind her.

He was back. She could sense him there, watching her. Even when his footsteps grew silent, she knew he was there. Rage ignited even as unease uncurled, the two blending in an unpleasant mix. She resented his presence, feared it, but had no real idea how to remove it. The best she could do was ignore it just as she had been, but she didn't know how long she could continue with that course, how long he would be satisfied to remain at a distance.

As she passed the graveyard, the shadows breathed and waited. She hurried on, resisting the urge to turn and search for him in the gloom.

Even once she reached the ward, she felt as though someone watched her here among the sick and dying as she moved between the beds, checking on the patients, taking note of glassy eyes or rapid breathing, offering water to those who asked.

She looked to each corner in turn. In one was a bucket and mop, in another a straight-backed chair. The third held a table and the fourth was empty. Nothing was out of place. There was no danger here unless it was the danger of human suffering and tragedy.

Moments later, two boys hauled in a massive cauldron of porridge and set it on the floor beside the square table. As Sarah drew near, she detected an acrid scent; the gruel had cooked on too hot a flame. One more unpleasant scent to add to the slurry. She was careful not to dip the ladle too deep or scrape the burnt gruel up from the bottom as she ladled it into small bowls and lined them in neat rows on the tray atop the table by her side.

With a swish of her black skirts, Elinor Bayley approached. She was a young widow, just a few years older than Sarah, and she had once confided that she regretted the loss of Mr. Bayley not at all. He had been forty years her senior, over-fond of drink, and—Sarah understood from the things that Elinor didn't say—a strong believer in physically disciplining his wife for any transgression, real or imagined.

During the first several weeks they had worked together, Sarah had been polite but reserved. Then one day, Elinor had thrown up her hands and said, "You must call me Elinor. And I shall call you Sarah. It's ridiculous that we should work together, changing linens stained with other people's sh—" She had pressed two fingers to her lips.

"Shite," Sarah had finished for her, unoffended.

"Quite," Elinor had replied. "It is ridiculous that we call each other Miss Lowell and Mrs. Bayley. We are friends. I am Elinor. You are Sarah." And that had been that.

Now Elinor turned and dipped her chin toward one of the beds, the gathered tufts of blond corkscrew curls on either side of her head bouncing. "Mrs. Cook's covered in bites. Bed bugs. And this morning the cockroaches are knee deep in the corners."

Sarah cut her a sidelong glance. "Knee deep?"

Elinor smiled, dimples in both cheeks. "Well, ankle deep. Just last week, the matron said we ought to hire a man like the one at Guy's Hospital to deal with the bugs."

"The matron's right, but we have not the funds," Sarah said.

"A sad truth." Elinor lined up three more empty bowls on the tray.

As Sarah ladled porridge and filled the bowls, she caught a flicker of movement from the corner of her eye. She glanced at the half open door to the hallway just in time to see the back of a black clad form—broad shouldered, long limbed, sun-bright hair drawn back and tied at his nape.

That glimpse was enough. She knew him.

Mr. Thayne.

Light in the darkness.

Her belly fluttered and danced, the sensation having nothing to do with ill ease, and everything to do with Killian Thayne.

With her head cricked to one side, she leaned back, just a little, trying to see the last of him. But he was gone, and she was left with only the faintest echo of his boot-heels on the floorboards.

She was both amused and embarrassed by her own behavior. She had no reason to crave the sight of him, no reason at all.

But reason or not, she *did* crave the sight of him, and she spent far too much time thinking about him. He was a mystery, a man who kept to himself, preferring the night and shadows over the daylight, and the company of his books to that of his fellows.

She found him both fascinating and frightening.

"What are you looking at?" Elinor asked.

"Cockroaches," Sarah said. "Knee deep."

Elinor snorted. "Oh, I think not, missy. You were—"

The bell tolled cutting off her words—once, twice, thrice—a solemn and sinister peal that carried through walls of ancient, crumbling plaster and floorboards of greasy, rotting wood. It rang out not to mark the time, but as a summons.

A moment later feet pounded in the hallway. Summoned, they came, burly men in stained coats. The attendants. Their footsteps echoed through walls and closed doors, down the dim corridor toward the surgical ward, heavy and ominous.

They came because there was no laudanum for the poor and so the attendants would hold the patient down and the surgeon would be quick, the blades sharp, the ligatures tight, but it would not be enough. It was never enough. The screams would come, the tears and pleas. But the surgeon would cut off the limb regardless. And for all that suffering, by tomorrow or the next day, the patient was as like as not to be dead.

It was not surgery itself that disturbed Sarah. She had assisted her father so often that she thought she could likely perform one herself, *longed* to perform one herself, to apply all he had taught her. It was the ineffectiveness, the limited options the surgeons could offer. They saved few and lost many, and that was what ate at her. She ought to be used to it by now, ought to have learned to slam the door against her horror and dismay at the futility of trying to save them all. But she had not, and that was no one's failing but her own.

"There are three on the list today," Elinor said, jerking her head in the general direction of the surgical ward as she hefted the tray with the bowls of porridge. "Bless their poor souls."

"Three?" Sarah asked as they moved between the beds, shoulder to shoulder in the narrow space as they handed out breakfast. "There's Mrs. Smith." Her two rotten fingers were to be cut away. An appropriate treatment. Their removal would mean that Mrs. Smith would live instead of die, and since the mangled digits were the fourth and fifth on her left hand, her life would not be so very different with eight fingers rather than ten. "And Mr. Riley." They were to take his right foot at the ankle. He'd slipped in the muddy road and a carriage had crushed the bones of his foot. There was really no choice. Not if he wanted to live. Both surgeries were to be done by Mr. Simon, the head surgeon. He was an unpleasant person but a competent surgeon. "But who is the third?"

"Mr. Scully's doing poorly." Elinor shook her head. "The blister on his stump burst, and he's been feverish the night through. Mr. Franks wants to cut away the rest of the limb at the hip."

"The hip?" Sarah asked. Such a high amputation was fraught with danger. The patient rarely survived, and in this case, Sarah was almost certain he would not. A week ago, the first surgery had taken his limb just below the knee. It had almost killed him. A second such intervention surely would.

"Pity they must do their grisly work there on the ward," Elinor said, stopping with the tray to let Sarah pass the bowls to the patients on either side. "My sister was at St. Thomas. In Southwark. For the cholera. Spent a week there, and glad she was for the mercury the doctor gave her. Do you know they have a real operating theatre? Built in the old herb garret of the church. They do their surgeries there. Imagine!"

"An operating theater? I cannot imagine," Sarah replied then asked, "How are you today, Mrs. Toombs?" as she waited for the patient to haul herself to a sitting position using the rope that was strung between two tall poles attached to the bed, one fore, one aft.

"A mite better," Mrs. Toombs said, smiling her toothless smile. "Yesterday, all I could do was lie here and cry. Thought I was done for for certain. Then last night Mr. Thayne came and had me drink something vile—" she made a face "—and then this morning I woke up feeling hungry. Isn't it a wonder?"

"And here I am with breakfast," Sarah said. "A happy circumstance."

After passing off the bowl and spoon, Sarah followed Elinor and thought about the operating theater—a grand thing, in her estimation. King's College had no such luxury. Surgeries took place on the ward, with the surgical and apothecary apprentices gathered tight around the table, and all the other patients watching and listening as the attendants held the patient down. Sarah's father had not been in favor of such public practice. He believed a calm mind and soul went a far way toward healing the body. He had argued that surgeries ought to be performed in a separate room, but few of his colleagues had been inclined to listen.

"Was it Mr. Thayne you were so interested in earlier? Was it him you watched through the doorway?" Elinor asked, her tone wary.

"I watched no one," Sarah said. Truth. She hadn't watched him. He had already been gone and she had only glimpsed his passage.

Elinor rested her hand on Sarah's arm. "He's a handsome devil, I'll give him that. But..."

Sarah said nothing, even when it was clear that Elinor waited for either a reaction or an invitation to continue. She offered no such invitation.

Finally, Elinor shook her head, curls bouncing, and sighed. "None of my affair, I suppose."

"There is no affair, so it can be neither none nor some," Sarah replied, hoping that was the end of that. It was one thing to admire the breadth of Mr. Thayne's shoulders or the timbre of his voice in her own private thoughts. Quite another to have such ponderings noticed by another.

Continuing along the row of beds, Sarah doled out her porridge to those well enough to eat it, and made silent note of those who were not, intending to return and assess their condition once she was done handing out the meal.

The situation was frustrating for her. She was a day nurse, in essence a domestic servant in the ward, charged with cleaning and serving meals and little more. The head nurse or the sisters under her supervision were responsible for direct patient care. On the surgical ward, the apprentices were tasked with the care of complicated cases. It ate at Sarah that she was capable of doing more, wanted to do more, but she was prohibited.

She had been at King's College for a month when she had braved the office of the matron to request additional duties and chores. She had worked by her father's side—both in his surgery and at the homes of patients—for almost her entire life, and she wanted to do more than work as a char. Her father's training should not go to waste. She knew well enough how to clean and dress a wound, lance a boil, treat a carbuncle. She wanted her knowledge to be put to good use.

But the matron had reminded her that she was lucky to have a position at all and that her presence here was suffered only on the memory of her father's good work and good name. Then she had sent Sarah on her way with an abrupt dismissal. Sarah was not so unwise as to have visited Matron with that request again.

When almost all the bowls had been distributed and only a handful of patients remained to be fed, Elinor offered, "I can finish this, Sarah. You go on to the surgical ward. They'll want someone to serve the meal there and gather the refuse. I'll be along when I'm done here."

With a nod, Sarah took her leave and moved along the dim corridor, her black skirt swishing as she walked.

4

Sarah had not even passed through the doors of the surgical ward before she heard an argument already in full vigor.

"I say we cut just above mid-thigh," came the voice of Mr. Simon, his tone tight with anger. "We can do it this very morning, before the other two."

Pausing in the doorway, she glanced at the group who stood by Mr. Scully's bedside. The man had been brought in more than a week ago. He had fractured his tibia and fibula in a fall, and the jagged shards had come through the skin. Open fractures were the most dangerous, the most prone to suppuration, and sure enough, within two days Mr. Scully's limb had become infected, and he was left with only two options. Amputation, or death.

He had chosen the former, and Mr. Simon had sawed off the limb below the knee.

For some days, Mr. Scully had done relatively well, but then his eyes had become glassy, his skin flushed and hot to the touch, and red streaks had begun to crawl up what was left of his leg.

Sarah had seen such an outcome many times before, and she knew it boded ill for the man's survival.

"And I say we must cut higher, closer to the hip," insisted Mr.

Franks. "Do you not smell it? Sickly sweet? It is not the rancid wet gangrene we deal with here, gentlemen, but the galloping gas gangrene. It will reach high into the healthy tissue and foul it as surely as I live and breathe."

There were murmurs of agreement from the group of gentlemen who hung on Mr. Franks' every word. And all this was said with Mr. Scully lying in the bed, mumbling and feverish.

Sarah hovered in the background, listening to the discussion as she began to ladle portions from a fresh kettle of porridge that had been brought from the kitchen by the same two lads who had lugged the first.

The gentlemen pressed together in a throng. Mr. Franks was the peacock of the group, his black frock coat the single somber element of his attire. He wore buff trousers and a red waistcoat over his protuberant belly, and a bright blue stock high about his neck.

His appearance contrasted starkly with Mr. Simon, a tall and gangly man, dressed all in black save for his white shirt, his bony wrists sticking out beyond his cuffs, his hands milk-white with long, slender fingers.

To his left was a young apothecary apprentice, his dark green frock coat and navy trousers covered by a white bib apron, the only one of the group who bothered in any way to protect his attire from the gore of the ward, or perhaps he sought to protect the patients from the unhealthy humors that might cling to his clothing.

Sarah's father had ever insisted that humors brought in from the street might create an unhealthy miasma for the patient. In her months working at King's College, she had seen much to support his theories.

She realized with a start that the apprentice was staring at her. He didn't look away when he saw that she had caught him. Instead, he lifted his brows and continued to stare. Unsettled, she turned her attention back to her task and when she glanced at him once more, he had looked away.

Sarah set down her ladle and angled closer to the bed until she could peer around the press of bodies to better see the patient for herself. His skin was as pasty as freshly boiled linens, slick with sweat.

His eyes were glassy, his breathing labored. She had no doubt that was she to have the opportunity to feel for his pulse, it would be rapid and wild.

There was a terrible odor coming from the stump. She could smell it even at this distance. Sarah disagreed with Mr. Franks on this. The smell was not sickly sweet, but the stink of rotting flesh. Thick, rancid pus oozed from the stump, and the free ends of the ligatures draped across the sheet, leaving trails of yellow-green suppuration.

"The hip it must be," said Mr. Franks.

"I beg to differ, sir. I must insist on mid-thigh," came Mr. Simon's sharp reply. "You well know that the higher the amputation the greater the risk of death."

"His risk is great enough from the spread of the poison. Do you not see it, man, crawling up his thigh like a spider?" Mr. Franks turned and looked about at his supporters, who murmured agreement.

He was wrong. The poison was not crawling up his thigh. It was well past that point, streaks of red extending all the way up, past his hip.

The patient, Mr. Scully, roused himself enough to look slowly back and forth between the doctors, his entire body trembling, his lips working but making no sound. Sarah wondered if he understood what they were saying, or if he was caught in a delirium brought on by the poison that was flowing through his body.

Off to one side, the attendants moved about, preparing the large wooden table for the operations to come, scattering fresh sawdust on the floor beneath to catch the blood that would drip down. There was only a curtain separating the table from the remainder of the ward.

On a smaller wooden bench were laid out the necessary implements. Sharp knives, some curved, some straight, designed to sweep clear through skin and muscle, down to the bone. An ebony handled saw. Petit's screw tourniquets. Curved needles. Tenaculum to grab the artery and allow for the silk ligature to tie it off. A basin.

How many times had she stood by her father's side and handed him each item as he needed it, no words exchanged, no request necessary?

From him, she had learned how to tighten the tourniquet, tie a ligature, even the appropriate way to cut flaps of skin and allow for healing by first intention.

Of course, she had never done a surgery on her own, but she had worked at her father's side for years, never thinking about whether she liked the role, whether she wanted to be there. She had been there because he needed her hands, because the patients needed the care, because she could not deny succor to any who suffered. It was not in her nature. And because she was good at it, her instincts sure and true. Her father had remarked on that often, even going so far as to occasionally follow a path she suggested instead of the one he had planned.

Then, abruptly, her father was gone. Dead. He had left her alone and destitute, forced to take a position at King's College as a day nurse, because there was no other option open to her. Well...not unless she wanted to stand on a corner dressed in bright colors with her bodice cut low, leaning against a post by the gin houses of Seven Dials.

Sarah was grateful that the physicians of King's College remembered her father with fond respect, and so recommended her to the matron for a position in the wards.

She had thought a great deal about her preferences since then, and she had realized that though her emotions rebelled against the suffering of the sick and injured, and the environment itself made her at times feel sad and drained and worn, she yearned to help these people, to offer comfort and solace and what little healing she could. What had begun as a path following in her father's footsteps simply because he expected it had become her own inclination somewhere in time. Had she been her father's son rather than his daughter, she would be one of the surgeons on this ward.

For an instant, she wondered what she might say if she were one of the surgeons standing by the bed. Not the high amputation; it was too dangerous. But given the red streaks that marked the path of the poison, she feared that the lower amputation would do no good at all. Neither path appeared to offer any better hope than doing nothing at all.

As the men continued their argument, Sarah sensed the patient's growing distress. With a cry, he reared up and peered around the crowd to lock his gaze on the operating table.

Thrashing, he turned toward Sarah, and she saw that his eyes were fever bright. He began to sob, deep, guttural sounds that she felt in the marrow of her bones. Then his gaze locked on her, his attention complete.

"Please," he said. "Do not let them do this. Do not."

She stood, frozen. All eyes turned in her direction, and she was caught like a rabbit in an open field. Her heart twisted in a tight, black knot. She had drawn attention to herself. There was real danger in that. What had possessed her to step up and insinuate herself at the edges of the group? It was far better to avoid notice, to go about her duties like a wraith. She could not afford their notice, could not afford to have one of them decide she was unwelcome here at King's College.

"Please," Mr. Scully begged. "You cannot understand what it was like to be cut like that, to feel as if time stopped in the instant of that agony, trapping me there. Never have I known such darkness, such despair. Never have I so truly believed that my maker had deserted me, left me in a cauldron of pain and suffering, left me there alone."

All around them, other patients shifted restlessly, disturbed by Mr. Scully's cries. Some called out, and some stayed stoically silent.

"Enough." A single word, spoken in a low, even tone. And it *was* enough, for the sounds settled and somehow, the tension in the ward eased.

Killian Thayne stepped through the door of the ward and made his way to the far side of Mr. Scully's bed. As was his habit, he was garbed all in black, the somber tone a contrast to the pale gold of his hair.

Slowly, he reached up to remove his spectacles. His hands were large, strong, his nails smooth and clean. The spectacles looked small and fragile in his grasp, yet he held them with the gentlest care as he folded the arms. After a moment, he placed them in the inside breast pocket of his impeccably cut coat. When he raised his head, his gaze slid past each of the surgeons in turn, to the attendants setting up the operating table, and finally to Sarah herself.

This was the first time she had ever seen him without his spectacles. His eyes were gray. Not the soft color of a dove, but the rough, turbulent shade of a raging winter storm. A powerful storm.

He held it leashed, that power.

And it made her shiver.

"Your thoughts?" Mr. Thayne asked, and Sarah's heart slammed against her ribs. He could not be asking her here, in front of all and sundry. He could not be drawing such attention to her.

Barely had those thoughts formed than he swung his gaze to a surgical apprentice and listened patiently while the man replied. Sarah sagged in relief. But even as she eased away from the group back toward the kettle of porridge, she thought that the question *had* been aimed at her, that Mr. Thayne would have liked to know her opinion on the matter, that he had turned away at the last second only out of deference to her position.

Answering his query would have been disastrous, for he was certainly the only one in the group who would want the opinion of a day nurse, a *woman*, though she had studied under her father for more years than any of the surgical apprentices here. Lifting her ladle, she feigned absorbed interest in her task.

From the corner of her eye, she caught Mr. Thayne staring at her for a heartbeat, then he looked down at the man in the bed and said, "Mr. Scully, you have an infection in the flesh of your stump, and a poison in the blood." His tone was calm, compassionate. "My companions suggest that if they do a second amputation, higher than the first, they might save your life."

The patient ceased his moaning and restless thrashing the moment Mr. Thayne turned his attention to him. Sarah had seen this before. Killian Thayne ever had a calming effect on the sick and dying.

She wondered at that, wondered how a man who caused such upheaval inside of *her* could so effortlessly soothe the emotions of those in physical torment.

"Mr. Simon argues for the thigh, Mr. Franks for the hip," he continued.

"I fear it will not save me," the patient said, surprisingly lucid, though his voice trembled. "I fear I will die regardless what they do now. I feel it. I feel the poison working through me, an evil humor. So, you tell me...which will save me, the higher or the lower? Or do they propose the cutting only as a means to show these apprentices the way of things?"

"I say," interjected Mr. Simon, his tone outraged. Then he exchanged a glance with Mr. Franks, and Sarah read the truth in that. They *were* inclined to insist upon the surgery in order to offer the learning experience to their apprentices, for how were prospective surgeons to know the way of things except by observation of the operations in question?

Though she understood the logic, the thought of seeing Mr. Scully —or any patient—subjected to such horror merely as a teaching tool revolted her.

As Mr. Scully raised his hand from the mattress, the limb shaking wildly, Mr. Thayne grasped it, his gaze never leaving the man's face. Sarah held her breath, waiting for his answer, wondering what he would say, for she suspected that he thought as she did, that it was far too late for Mr. Scully, that no intervention would save this man's life.

Mr. Simon and Mr. Franks interjected with, "I say," and "Here now," but it mattered not. The patient's entire focus was on Killian Thayne's eyes.

"Mr. Simon truly believes he can save you," Mr. Thayne said. He made no mention of Mr. Franks.

"But do *you* believe it?" Mr. Scully asked.

The entire ward stilled, hanging on Killian Thayne's reply. But when he spoke it was to offer a question rather than an answer.

"You say that you fear you will die regardless, but is it death you fear, sir?" Mr. Thayne's voice was low, smooth. Enticing. Luring the true secrets of the patient's deepest deliberations.

Sarah thought that should he ask *her* a question in that tone, with that intent look fixed upon her, she would surely bare the entirety of her heart and soul.

"Fear death?" Mr. Scully frowned and pondered that for an instant, then he went on, speaking with unexpected eloquence for one who had been mired for days in the depths of delirium. "No. I do not fear it. My wife has passed on ahead of me, and all four of my sons. I've little left here, and I suppose—" he shot a glance at Mr. Simon "—that no matter where they make their barbarous cut, I shall die regardless. I can feel the weight of death's touch on my shoulder."

"Yes," Mr. Thayne agreed. "Death's touch is upon you."

The gaggle of murmuring apprentices fell silent at the low-spoken pronouncement.

Sarah swallowed, unnerved, for it was Mr. Thayne's free hand that rested upon Mr. Scully's shoulder.

"I do not want the surgery. Let death come," the patient said, vehement. "You asked if it is death I fear? Not at all. I fear they'll cut me in bits and pieces until there's no more of me to cut. But I am already dead. There's just the shell of me what's got to give up the spirit. I feel it inside of me, the poison. I feel it."

His words were clear and certain, and again Sarah could not help but wonder at that, at his lucidity of the moment. He had been nothing of the sort for days now, instead rambling and moaning and insisting he saw his wife sitting at the foot of his bed, talking to her, though she had been dead these past four years.

She had the unexpected thought that it was Mr. Thayne—his touch on the man's shoulder; the unwavering connection of his gaze—that steadied him. Rationality argued against the possibility, but Sarah could not discount it.

"You have no say here, Thayne," Mr. Franks interjected, spittle flying from his lips as his agitation spurred his words. "The patient is not yours, and I will thank you to mind yourself."

"And the *limb* is not *yours*," Mr. Thayne replied, unperturbed. His tone was ice and steel and not one of them dared to interject or voice objection. His lips turned, as though he found the other surgeon amusing or, perhaps, contemptible. "Look here—" he gestured to the red streaks on the patient's limb "—and here. Even taking the leg at the hip will not stop the spread." It had already moved too far. They could all see it.

For a long moment, no one spoke, then Mr. Simon offered a curt nod of agreement.

Mr. Thayne turned to him. "We both know that your proposed intervention will not succeed." He glanced at Mr. Franks. "And yours is more likely to kill than to cure. The patient has said he has no wish for your further surgical involvement, and I am of the opinion that his decision is wise." He paused. "Can you tell me that you have even a marginal hope of saving his life with your knives and saws?"

Mr. Simon swallowed, glanced at the patient, and said, "There is always hope," though his tone and expression suggested he harbored none.

"Is there?' Mr. Thayne asked.

Yes, Sarah wanted to say. *There is always hope. Without hope, we are nothing.* But perhaps hope took different forms and when the hope for survival was gone, one could hope for a gentle passing from this life to the next. Had her father known a gentle passing beneath the dark and oily surface of the Thames?

When Mr. Simon made no reply, Mr. Thayne continued. "If you were the one lying in this bed, what would you choose?" There was a silky threat in his tone.

Mr. Simon glanced at Mr. Franks, opened his mouth, and then closed it without uttering a word.

Sarah's gaze slid back and forth between the two, then Mr. Thayne made a smooth gesture of dismissal and turned to the matron who stood in the doorway. "Offer him as much gin as he can swallow. Laudanum, if you have it. Dull the pain as best you can, and let him make this journey in whatever peace he can find."

With that, he returned his attention to the man on the bed, leaning low to say something near his ear. Sarah could hear none of it, and from the expressions on the faces of the group of apprentices and surgeons, they could hear nothing of the exchange either. It irked them. That much was obvious.

Whatever quiet words Mr. Thayne offered, they had an immediate further calming effect on the patient, a lessening of visible agitation. Mr. Scully's eyes slid shut and the tension in his body eased.

Surprised, Sarah wondered if Mr. Thayne were a mesmerist.

Before his death, her father had taken her to see a public demonstration put on by the mesmerist John Elliotson. He had laid his hands upon a woman and sent her into catalepsy from which loud noises and even needles poked into her skin had not roused her. Now, Sarah could not help but note the similarities between Elliotson's display and the way that Mr. Scully eased so completely from distress into relaxation.

Regardless of the reason, she was glad that Mr. Thayne's presence offered some relief for the patient's suffering, and she was glad, too, that he was here to speak against the futile amputation of the remainder of the limb. The interventions of mortals could not change the outcome for Mr. Scully. If he was destined to live, it would be a heavenly intervention that made it so.

Again, Mr. Thayne's gaze slid to hers, and he made a small nod, as though he knew and understood her thoughts. As though they shared some sort of collusion.

Awareness shivered through her, an instant of connection.

Mr. Simon and Mr. Franks walked on, followed by their entourage.

Moving to Mr. Scully's side, Sarah wet the corner of a cloth and dabbed moisture along his cracked lips. He opened his eyes, and murmured, "Sit with me for a bit, Martha. Sit with me for a bit and sing to me the way you sang to our babes when they were small." He caught her wrist, his grasp weak as he frowned up at her as though he was trying to remember who she was. At length, he said, "He made the arrangements as I asked. He's bought you passage to Edinburgh, to your sister. You needn't stay here alone. He's a good one, Martha. A good one. I had not the coin to pay your way, but he said it was of no concern."

Sarah frowned, trying to make sense of his words. Martha—Mr. Scully's wife—was dead... She glanced at Mr. Thayne then returned her gaze to Mr. Scully. "Whom do you send to Edinburgh?" she asked.

He frowned and then his expression cleared. "My sister. I send my sister to Martha's sister so neither needs be alone."

Of course. His sister, Mary. She sold posies during the day, but Sarah had seen her here beside his bed in the evenings; they'd spoken briefly.

He shifted restlessly and scratched vigorously first at his neck, then at his arm. "Itchy," he muttered, then made a watery laugh. "Sleep tight. Don't let the bedbugs bite." He closed his eyes again and, after a moment, fell into fitful slumber.

She raised her gaze to Mr. Thayne and found him watching her.

"The fever makes his skin itch," she murmured, compelled to fill the silence. "Or the bedbugs."

He studied her face in silence, and his straight, dark gold brows drew together, as though he puzzled through some particular matter.

She felt undone by that look, felt that with it he reached beyond her skin and looked deep inside her heart and soul.

"Your thoughts?" he asked.

So, she had been right. He *did* want to hear her opinion. After making certain there was no one close enough to overhear, she rested her fingers on the side of Mr. Scully's throat, counting his pulse, watching the rise and fall of his chest. "Fever. Rapid breathing. Rapid pulse." She looked up. "He is confused and disoriented. I saw earlier that the putrefaction and rot have spread past the hip. There are red and purple streaks all the way to his waist. I do not think there is much we can do but make him as comfortable as possible."

Mr. Thayne nodded. "If you had been responsible for his care from the moment he arrived, what would you have done?"

Sarah wet her lips. "I would have amputated. But I would have first boiled the linens for his bed and the cloth used for dressing the wound. I would have made my cut a little higher, above the infection. My father taught me that it is essential to remove as much damaged tissue as possible. I would have changed the dressing more frequently. And—" She hesitated to say the next bit. He would think her mad.

"Go on," he said, a command.

"And directly after the amputation I would have applied molding bread before the dressing." There. She had said it. She waited for him to dismiss her words.

Instead, he said, "Molding bread? Why?"

In for a penny, in for a pound. Her chin kicked up. "My father learned the technique from a woman in Scotland years ago. He had traveled to Edinburgh to attend the anatomy lectures of Robert Knox and he stayed on to travel the countryside. The woman was a healer. The folk in her village both respected and feared her skill. She told my father the mold lessened putrefaction. She gave him a jar as a parting gift. When I was small, it was my job to feed it."

"Your job to feed it? Now there's an image." The corners of Mr. Thayne's lips lifted. Sarah stared at his mouth. *She* had elicited that tiny smile. It was for her and her alone.

She could not help but smile in return. "I added stale crusts of bread and the mold proliferated. When my father used it up in treatment, I fed it more bread."

He made a soft laugh. "An odd pet."

"It was," she said, his laughter warming her even more than his smile.

"And did the mold save your father's patients?"

"Some," Sarah said as she glanced about once more. The matron watched her from across the ward, arms crossed, a frown clouding her features.

Mr. Thayne followed her gaze and intuited the situation. With a dip of his chin, he said, "We will speak of your pet another day. I leave the patient in your most competent care, Miss Lowell."

His words shimmered through her, and she wondered if he knew how much she valued his acknowledgment of her skill. *She* knew she was competent. It wasn't that she needed his validation, but acknowledgment was...nice.

As Mr. Thayne turned to leave, Mr. Scully lurched up and caught hold of his frock coat, tightening his fingers in the material so that his knuckles showed white.

"Please," he begged, his voice slurred, as though he had already been well dosed with the gin Mr. Thayne had recommended. "Please do it for me. Do it quick. With a knife, or some other way. Fast and clean. This is a terrible suffering, and we both know they'll only come again. What if you are not here to speak for me? What if they drag me to that table and hold me down and cut my flesh? I do not want to die that way, sawed into sections like wood for a fire." He paused, and then said in a clear, ringing voice, "Kill me and be done with it. You know the way of it, Mr. Thayne."

A heavy hush fell on the ward. Many eyes watched the scene unfold and many ears listened.

Mr. Thayne held the man's gaze for a moment, his expression ruthlessly neutral. "Sleep now," he said. Then he reached into his pocket, withdrew his bottle-green spectacles, and slid them on to hide his eyes.

A mask, Sarah thought. A wall.

With a groan, Mr. Scully loosened his hold and dropped his hand back to the sheets, his eyes rolling back and his lids lowering. His hand slid down to hang at an uncomfortable angle, and Sarah moved forward to set it back on the bed.

When she looked up once more, a single shaft of light broke through the grime of the window to cut across the floor exactly where Mr. Thayne had stood.

But he was gone. Disappeared. His passage silent as the mist.

5

Bergen, Norway, 1349

K<small>JELL WATCHED THE STRANGER FALL TO ASH, WATCHED HIS CLOTHES</small> *crumple empty to the ground, and he understood nothing. None of this was real. Everything—the stranger, his mother's death, the pain in his wrist—was but a fever dream, a delirium. That was the only explanation. He tried to move, to rise, but he was weak and weighted by despair.*

The pain in his gut bloomed, a dark flower, and spread like a poison to his limbs, his head. He writhed and cried out for hours upon hours.

It was the smell that woke him, the smell of death, like nothing he had ever experienced. The smell, the sounds, the feeling of his clothing on his body, all familiar yet not. His wrist no longer pained him. He examined it to find no wound.

He must have slept and in that sleep, he must have dreamed the stranger, his mother's death, even the sunrise.

The day had passed. It was night now, and the room was cold. The fire had long since gone out. But the cold was merely a fact, not a discomfort. His teeth did not chatter; his limbs did not tremble. He raised his hand and stared at his fingers, feeling as if he had never seen them before. The small hairs on his forearm were a wonder, the shape of his nails inexplicably fascinating, the sinew and muscle beneath his skin a symphony of movement. It took some time for him to remember to think of anything else.

He rolled to his side and pushed up to a sitting position. His family was all around him, but they were gone. Dead. His father, his sisters, his brother, his—

His mother lay where the stranger had left her, her throat torn open.

No dream. It was real. The stranger had been real.

Kjell's heart broke, shattered, and he yelled and railed even as he knew it wouldn't bring her back.

He knew not how long he remained in that room. He brushed his sisters' hair. He hugged his brother's lifeless body in his arms. He wept tears of blood. The sun rose again and he hissed at the agony it caused, though little enough filtered through the animal skins that covered the windows. He crawled to his father's bed and yanked off the blanket and spent the day hiding beneath it while the sun found small ways to poke through and burn him.

It had burned the stranger to ash.

He would be wary of the sun.

Then it was night once more, cool soothing night and he was hungry, a strange hunger that could not be satisfied by food. In fact, the pickled fish and cheese and bread he tried to consume made him sick. And still, the hunger persisted, gnawing at him. It was not merely a growl or a twist in his belly. The hunger consumed him, lacing every breath, every movement of his limbs. He felt hollow, anxious, his skin too tight, his bones aching and empty.

He set fire to his childhood home, burning the bodies of his family, his heart heavy. The smell of smoke, the heat of the flames, they were as they had always been and yet they were new and foreign. Everything was different. Everything was familiar but not, as if he had never before smelled fire, never before watched tongues of fire dance and writhe. The fire burned down to ash and as he sensed the coming dawn clawing at his skin, he wrapped himself in furs and tunneled under the ash to wait out the sun.

He walked that night. In the morning, he felt dawn's approach, felt it on his skin and in his soul, an itch that grew into a burning sting that grew into a blazing pain. And that with only the first hint dusting the horizon. That day he hid in a farmhouse with the bodies of the dead. It was everywhere, the plague. It killed all those it touched.

He found food and, ravenous, he again stuffed salted fish into his mouth, chewed, swallowed. The taste was vile. The fish refused to remain in his belly. And he thought of the stranger hunched over his mother's throat, of the sounds of slurping and guzzling. And he knew.

This all-consuming, mindless hunger would not be slaked by fish or meat or bread. He huddled in the house as the sunlight reached across the floor toward him, and he thought of walking to greet it as the stranger had.

He thought it, but he did not do it.

He walked on, hiding from the sun each day, knowing that he must find a way to feed, horrified by what he knew he must do in order to survive.

On the fifth night, he could barely walk, so consuming was his hunger. It clawed at his insides and made his thoughts veer from reason. He was near mindless, dragging one foot before the next, searching, searching. And then a scent carried on the wind, the scent of ambrosia, so rich and delicious he almost wept. He followed the smell, dizzy with hunger until he came upon a man huddled beneath layers of warm fur, a small fire burning before him.

The man glanced up as Kjell stepped from the trees toward the flames. He looked weary and spent, and there was blood on his temple and on his cheek. Kjell stared at the blood, lured in a way he had never been before, not by food or drink or even a woman. This was something else entirely.

"Come no closer," the man said. "I am sick. It is plague." He turned his head and coughed until blood stained the ground. Kjell trembled where he stood, fighting a vicious battle within himself. "I will likely be dead by morning," the man continued. "Stay back unless you wish the same for yourself."

Kjell swallowed. He would kill this man in a moment. He would take his blood and his life. He should at least know his first victim's name. Beastly hunger roaring inside him, and he forced himself to fight against it, to ask, "What is your name?"

The man frowned and said, "Thayne. Killian Thayne."

And then Kjell was upon him, tearing open his throat with his teeth, drinking his fill, taking the life of Killian Thayne, hating himself for it even as he licked at every last drop, the taste more wondrous than anything he had ever known, and he acknowledged that he would do it again and again, that he would feed, that he would live.

He was not the boy he had been. He was reborn that night as the life of his prey slipped away.

Days later, when he reached the harbor, he boarded a ship to England under the name of the first man whose life he had stolen. He was Kjell no longer; he was Killian Thayne.

❧ 6 ❧

Sarah rolled to her side in her tiny bed, neither asleep nor awake, but somewhere in between. The room was cold. She lay beneath her sheets, two thin blankets, and her cloak, which she had spread over top for extra warmth. Her lids fluttered open. She had dreamed of sunshine and a picnic with her father, but she saw only darkness now.

Restless, she rolled again, tired, so tired. A hand, warm and gentle, settled on her brow and stroked her hair back from her face.

"Sleep," a man's voice said. "Sleep now, Sarah. Dream sweet dreams."

A man's voice, here in her room. A man's hand on her brow. That couldn't be right. She knew that voice. It was...

Sleep reached for her and pulled her deep.

∽

EARLY THE FOLLOWING MORNING, SARAH MADE HER WAY ALONG THE corridor of King's College, shadows and moonlight creeping across the floor in an alternating pattern of light and dark stripes. Her steps quick and sure, she went directly to the surgical ward, anxious to check on Mr. Scully. He had clung to life throughout the previous day, crying out, moaning, growing increasingly ill. He had been feverish and lost in a world of his own making. Each time Sarah had looked in on him he had not recognized her, mistaking her for his dead wife.

Now, she wondered if he had lived through the night.

She paused in the doorway of the ward, her gaze sliding to Mr. Scully's bed. There came a rushing sound, like wings beating, or a cloak flapping in the wind. She took a single step forward, then froze and made a startled gasp.

Outlined on the far wall was a looming shadow in the shape of a man, his height and breadth exaggerated and magnified.

A shadow with no source.

She was the only upright person in the ward. Everyone else lay supine on their beds. There was no man to cast such a shadow. Her blood chilled and her gaze skittered about the room to make certain she was not mistaken.

When she looked once more at the wall, the shadow was gone, disappeared.

But the fine hairs that rose at her nape and the clammy fingers oozing across her skin made her certain that she had not imagined it, and that whoever—*whatever*—had cast the dark silhouette yet hovered, unseen, in the gloom.

Pressing her palm flat against her breastbone, she tried to will both her racing pulse and her galloping imagination under control. Either there was someone here or there wasn't, and she meant to determine which it was. Squaring her shoulders, she went and lifted the mop from the bucket that stood in the corner. The handle would do as a weapon if needs must. Then she walked the perimeter of the room and found no one there.

Still, she could not discount what she had seen. Someone had been in the ward and gone to great lengths to remain anonymous.

After returning the mop to its place, she went to Mr. Scully's bed.

"Mr. Scully," she whispered. "Mr. Scully, how do you this morn?"

He lay quiet and still.

But there was *something* about the way he was arranged in repose...something both macabre and familiar. His head lolled to one side, his arms hanging over the edges of the bed.

Breathing too fast, she took a step closer.

A patient called out to her, but she did not so much as turn her head, for her entire focus was on the sight of Mr. Scully's form, a lump beneath stained and frayed sheets. Not moving. Not breathing.

The smell hit her, a heavy slap of urine and excrement.

Dead. He was dead. Released from his pain.

His eyes were closed. Sarah reached down and lifted his arm. His wrist was torn open, a jagged, gaping wound, the edges of skin and muscle shredded to reveal the whitish tendons of the long flexor muscles that stretched to his fingers.

There was no blood.

Despite the torn edges of the hole at his wrist and the depth of the wound, there was not a single crimson drop upon the sheet or the floor beneath.

For a moment, she could not breathe, could not think, and then she forced herself to lower his arm to the bed, to sharpen her attention, to determine exactly what it was that whispered to her to look closer.

Slowly, she walked all the way around the bed, aware that the patients on the ward were stirring, asking for water, for food, for a moment of comfort. Soon, someone else would hear the commotion, and they would come, they would see...

What? They would see what?

The body of a man who had been destined to die?

Yes. But the manner of said death was both bizarre and disturbing.

The fourth such death here at King's College.

She shivered.

"Miss Lowell? Is aught amiss?"

She heard the voice as though it came to her through a long, narrow tunnel.

Turning, she faced him, Killian Thayne, tall and broad and unsmiling. He stood close enough to touch, dressed all in black, like a shadow, his eyes hidden behind the dark glass of his spectacles.

"He is dead," she said, her tongue like leather in her mouth. "Mr. Scully is dead."

"An expected outcome." He paused "Yet you are distressed by his passing."

"By the *mode* of his passing," she said in a rush, then wondered that she could be so foolish.

Someone, a man, had been here earlier. She had seen his shadow. A large shadow cast by a tall man.

And here was Killian Thayne standing before her, broad and tall. Had he sat by Mr. Scully's bed this morn just as he had sat by another patient's bedside on a morning weeks past, another patient who had died with the same strange and inexplicable wounds?

"Let me see." Mr. Thayne stepped around her and then around the bed to the far side. He stared at Mr. Scully's sprawled form for a long moment.

Wrapping her arms around her waist, Sarah watched him. His expression was unperturbed, his posture relaxed, but something felt off. Then she realized his lips had drawn taut. That was the only sign of his displeasure.

He turned to face her once more and after a long moment said, "You are pale. Have you eaten today?"

"I—" She hadn't. Usually, she bought a bowl of salop from a street vendor near the lodging house, but this morning she had taken a different route to King's College, one that did not carry her past the old woman and her still. She had hoped that by varying her route she might evade the one who stalked her. A foolish hope. He had been behind her, clinging to the darkness, his footsteps keeping time with her own.

Mr. Thayne made a sound of frustration. "Have you brought food with you? Or do you intend to work the day through with nothing in your belly?"

It would be neither the first time nor the last. But that was none of his affair. She lifted her chin. "A man is dead."

Silence hung between them. "Fetch a stretcher," Mr. Thayne instructed, his voice soft. "I shall wrap him in a sheet."

"I can summon one of the other nurses to help me." She wondered why he offered to do this chore himself. Surgeons were not responsible for wrapping the dead.

Only for killing them.

She shuddered at the thought. What was it about Mr. Thayne that made her mind travel such a path? She knew that the physicians and surgeons at King's College did the best they could. That more than half the surgical patients died was a fact indisputably assigned to every hospital in the city.

But as she watched Mr. Thayne where he stood looming over Mr. Scully's corpse, she wondered how it was that he had been present at two such similar deaths. No...not two. Four. He had been nearby when each of the four patients had been found with their wrists torn open, and the bloody pool that ought to have accompanied such injury inexplicably absent.

He looked at her in the dim light, his eyes hidden behind his spectacles. She had the fanciful thought that he could see as deep as her soul, while she could see only the mask he chose to don.

Who—*what*—did he hide behind that mask?

Sarah took a small step back. She stopped herself from taking another, disturbed by her own wariness.

What was she thinking? Mr. Thayne was a healer. He spent an inordinate amount of time at the hospital. More than any of the other surgeons. He was dedicated to his patients. She had witnessed his care and kindness in the months she had worked these wards. Was she now to imagine that he had killed four people by tearing open their wrists? To what purpose? What end?

Confusion buffeted her, and she was appalled by her own thoughts, disdainful of them. She could not think why she allowed her mind to travel such a path.

"There is no blood," she said, challenge in her tone. *Explain that if you can, Mr. Thayne.*

"So I see," he replied, too savvy to take the bait.

"What do you know of this?"

His expression did not change. "I know that a man is dead. All else would be mere supposition or conjecture."

"Is it some sort of experiment? A study of the congealing properties of blood or..." She could think of nothing to add.

"A question or an accusation?" His tone was as calm as it had been a moment past, and there was nothing to suggest that her answer mattered in any special way. But it did. It mattered to her and she thought it mattered to him.

She categorized the facts in her mind, weighing truths and suppositions. She did not believe he had done these vile deeds. Not because she was foolishly blinded by her infatuation, but because logic decried that such an intelligent, thoughtful man would carry out such heinous crimes in a manner that could easily link them to him. "It was a question," she said at last.

Before he could respond there came a shocked cry. "Oh, my word. Another one with his wrist looking like he's been chewed by a beast," Elinor exclaimed, her palm pressed to the base of her throat. She reared back and looked about, her gaze pausing first on Sarah, then on Mr. Thayne. She paled as she looked at him, and blurted, "You were here. When the others died..."

"I was, yes." He made no effort to disagree, his tone calm and even. "I am a surgeon in this hospital—" he made a small, sardonic smile "—and am expected to attend on occasion."

He appeared to take no umbrage at Elinor's accusations.

"But you were there *every* time. No one else. Only you," Elinor whispered in horror, and the patients in the neighboring beds began to pick up the words and repeat them anew.

For an instant, Sarah felt a dizzying disconnection at the oddity of the situation. Here they stood among beds that held people whose limbs had been sawed off, whose skulls had been trephined, who suffered all manner of terrible wounds, yet the sight of a torn wrist elicited such horror and dismay.

Because there *was* something sinister about Mr. Scully's wound. It was not clean. It was not a slash or a cut made with a precise instrument. As Elinor had said, it *did* look as though an animal had chewed it open. One would think that a pool of blood would be cause for horror, yet the absence made the wound so much worse. She could not think of any injury or disease that left one drained of blood.

The murmurs in the ward grew and swelled.

Sarah turned to Mr. Thayne, and said, "Please do not let us delay you, sir. Mrs. Bayley and I can see to Mr. Scully. I am certain you have other things to occupy your attention."

His brows rose and again his lips curved in a hard, sardonic smile. She thought he might answer her, might argue, might chastise. But he only asked, "I have been dismissed, have I?" He made a shallow bow. "Then I bid you good morning."

He strode away, his long limbs eating the distance to the door. Sarah could not stop herself turning her head to watch him go.

And all around her, the whispers continued.

Elinor squeezed Sarah's shoulder.

"He didn't do this," Sarah said.

"How do you know?"

Sarah positioned Mr. Scully's arms so they lay crossed on his chest. "I know."

Elinor sighed. "I'll wrap him. You fetch a stretcher."

When Sarah returned, she found that Elinor had been shooed off to the side. Both Mr. Simon and Mr. Franks stood by the edge of the bed, along with the matron. The three were involved in an intense whispered discussion with much gesticulation and wary glances cast about. Mr. Simon rounded the bed, lifted Mr. Scully's savaged arm and spoke in a low, fervent tone. The content of his comments was lost to Sarah's ears, obscured by the general hubbub of the ward.

Her movements made awkward by the stretcher, she inched closer to the small group.

"It is Thayne's doing," Mr. Simon insisted, the words resonating with tension. "We all know it. He attended each of the four deaths, and we had words over the care of each of the four victims. Does no one else wonder at the strange coincidence?"

"What do you suggest, sir?" asked Mr. Franks. "That he bled the man dry? To what end?" His voice lowered still more. "Do you accuse him of murder?"

Sarah stifled a gasp, the sound faint in comparison to Elinor's huffing exclamation of dismay.

"I make no accusation." Mr. Simon offered a sneering, ugly smile. "I state only facts. Thayne disagreed with the treatment of each patient. He insisted that there was no hope for recovery and that death was the definitive outcome." He paused dramatically and looked about at the neighboring beds as though attempting to be circumspect. A carefully structured ploy, for had that been his genuine intent, he would have taken this discourse to a more private venue. "Thayne was the last to see this man alive. It is well past time for us to summon the authorities."

Sarah could not say what possessed her in that moment, but she stepped forward as though in a trance, and spoke in Mr. Thayne's defense.

"Sir," she said. "I was here when Mr. Scully died. Mr. Thayne arrived only later." Not precisely the truth, but not exactly a lie, either. Mr. Thayne *had* arrived later...at least, she thought he had, for she could not say whose shadow she had seen; it could have been his. And as to her assertion that she had been here when Mr. Scully expired, well, she had likely been on the premises somewhere, though not at his bedside. Gently bending the truth was a far cry from breaking it. "And perhaps his wound might be explained by the bugs."

They all stared at her.

"He was...That is..." She wet her lips.

"What place have you in this discussion, Miss Lowell?" Mr. Simon demanded with enough force and fury that Sarah almost silenced herself.

Drawing her courage about her like a cloak, she forced herself to continue in a calm and even manner. "Mr. Scully was complaining yesterday that his skin itched. He said it was bedbugs, and perhaps the added distress of the fever and the infection spreading through his body made him scratch. Could the injuries to his wrist be excoriation? Self-inflicted as he sought to ease the itch?"

There was urgency in her defense; she was driven to offer an alibi for Mr. Thayne. Something inside her would not let them mark him as a murderer.

"You suggest that each of the four patients who died in this exact manner tore at their own skin, driven mad by the itch?" Mr. Franks scoffed.

"Matron said we ought to hire a man to see to the bugs, the way they have at St. Thomas and other hospitals." Sarah cut a glance at the other woman, who hesitated for an instant and then nodded her agreement.

"But to tear the skin clean through? And the blood vessels, as well?" Mr. Franks folded his hands across his ample belly and peered down his nose at her.

Sarah bit her lip. The possibility was ludicrous, but she had set herself on this path and now saw no clear way to change course. Her thoughts skittered this way and that as she tried to summon an appropriate reply.

"Let us examine his body for signs of excoriation," came Mr. Thayne's voice from close behind her. She spun so quickly that she nearly unbalanced herself.

He had arrived just in time to save her from her attempt to save him.

Calm and steady, his gaze met hers for an instant, his green tinted spectacles nowhere to be seen. She almost wished that he was wearing them, for they offered some protection from his piercing, too-knowing gaze. She had defended him, bent the truth for him. It was a dangerous path she had chosen.

"Yes, let us examine for such signs," snarled Mr. Simon, and with little care for propriety or respect, he reached down and yanked aside the neck of the nightshirt that covered Mr. Scully's pale torso. Deep runnels were gouged in his chest from where he had, indeed, scratched himself raw.

His face a mask of shock, Mr. Simon jerked back and let go his hold on the cloth. "It means nothing."

Mr. Franks shook his head and hooked his thumbs in his lapels. "It means a great deal."

"It does not explain the lack of blood."

"The poison from his wound would explain it," Mr. Franks said.

It would not, but Sarah had no intention of saying so. In this moment, she was immensely glad of Mr. Franks' contrary nature. If Mr. Simon claimed the sky was blue, then Mr. Franks would argue that it was green, simply because he could not help himself. A boon, under the circumstances, for it offered her an unexpected ally.

With everyone's attention locked on this new evidence, Mr. Thayne leaned in and spoke for her ears alone.

"My champion, Miss Lowell?" He sounded amused.

"Only the voice of reason," she whispered in return. "They were ready to name you a ravening beast that chewed flesh and drank blood."

When no reply was immediately forthcoming, she glanced back at him over her shoulder and found him far too close for either propriety or comfort. Too tall. Too broad. Too male.

Golden stubble dusted his jaw and his sun-bright hair had come free of its tie to fall in loose, thick waves.

"A ravening beast," he mused, and his lips curved in a dark smile. "Perhaps the descriptor is fitting." There was no sarcasm in his tone.

"Why would you say that?" she demanded.

"People are often not what they appear."

His eyes glittered, gray and brooding as a storm-chased sky, myriad emotions reflected in their silvered depths. Dark emotions. Loneliness. Regret. Sadness. Attraction. Or perhaps she only saw the things that dwelled in the shadowed corners of her own heart and soul.

She turned forward once more to stare straight ahead at Mr. Simon and Mr. Franks who bickered back and forth like two boys in short pants.

Buffeted by both confusion and dismay, she heard not a word of their discourse.

Mr. Thayne leaned in again and whispered, "Thank you," his breath fanning her cheek.

People are often not what they appear. With the heat and leashed threat of Killian Thayne so close at her back, she had the strange thought that he was not at all as he appeared, that the calm and controlled face he presented the world was not his true nature. That there was something inside of him, something dangerous and barely restrained.

That perhaps the label of beast was most apt.

But not *ravening.*

No, Killian Thayne would be more of a patient predator, one that watched and waited.

7

Only one attendant came to carry Mr. Scully away, which meant either Sarah or Elinor would need to haul the other end of the stretcher.

"Would you rather fetch linens and make up the bed or lift and carry?" Elinor asked.

"Linens," Sarah said with a glance at the bed. Another poor soul would arrive soon to take that spot, to lie moaning in pain, or stoically white-lipped.

That was the part she found difficult. She had little enough to offer the patients save for a cool hand on their brow or a cup of water or gin. The physicians doled out laudanum with a miserly fist when there was any to be had at all, for the cost was dear. So the patients suffered, and that suffering wore at her. She longed for a way to alleviate it.

She paused only long enough to wash her hands in the basin at the side of the ward. Others had commented on her obsession with cleanliness, including Mr. Franks and the matron. Mostly, the nurses washed not at all, and the surgeons only after a messy surgery to clean away the blood and gore. But Sarah's father had thought it important to wash both before and after patient care. He had believed that miasma was the source of illness, foul smell taking root and causing disease, and so he had insisted on cleanliness to curb fetid smells.

A mouse scurried in the shadows as she made her way along the wide corridor, the noise and clamor of the wards fading behind her. Slowing her pace, she turned down a narrower hallway and, finally, stepped into a small, dark alcove that housed the storage closet. The door was an ill-fitting slab of wood that stuck fast until she pulled hard, and then it scraped along the floor with a grating rasp.

She stared into the interior of the closet and thought that she ought to have brought a candle for there were no windows in the alcove or in the short, narrow hallway that led to it. The linens were on the middle shelf, a low stack of oft-mended, yellowed cloths that had been scrubbed and boiled time and again, and still bore the stains of many uses.

As Sarah stepped into the storage closet, a shush of sound behind her made her turn. She peered into the gloom but saw nothing more than dust and shadows. Then a mouse scurried across the floor and disappeared into a hole on the opposite wall.

Feeling foolish, she turned back to her task, stacking sheets and choosing several tallow candles to add to her pile. An eerie sensation tickled the fine hairs at her nape and again she heard a whooshing sound. She set down the gathered items on the shelf and turned to face the hallway.

"Hello," she called, feeling both wary and foolish.

A long, thin shadow stretched across the floor, stopping at the closet threshold.

Footsteps sounded from the distant corridor.

With a groan, the door of the closet swung shut, trapping her in the dark.

For an instant, she stood motionless, heart pounding, blood rushing in her ears. Then she placed both palms against the door and shoved, expecting it to be stuck or locked. It swung open with ease.

Sarah surged into the alcove then the narrow hallway. No one was there.

The wind caught her hair, pulling strands free of her pins. She spun to see that a window in the main corridor was open, the drapery flapping.

With a shake of her head and a self-deprecating laugh, she went to drag the window shut and ensure the latch was set. Then she returned to the closet where she added a stack of torn strips of cloth to act as bandages, for she had noticed that the stores in the ward were depleted.

Again, came the sensation that there was someone behind her, yet it was different than what she had felt earlier. Perhaps it was the faint scent of citrus that gave him away. *Killian.*

Her heart thudded in her breast and the walls of the small closet seemed to move closer still. It was not fear that touched her now; it was something else, something bigger and stronger, a stirring excitement that raced through her veins, dangerous and alluring at once.

Resting her hands on the shelf, she swallowed, struggling to gather her wayward emotions. If she turned, he would be only a hand span away, and she would...What? Dare to touch him? To lay her hand on his arm and know the strength of him?

Strange how this moment so closely resembled a thousand others. The difference was, *those* moments had taken place in her dreams, or in the waking daze as she first broke from slumber's embrace, alone in her bed, her thoughts focused on imagined shared moments where Killian came to her as a lover would.

The touch of his hand on her cheek. The scent of his skin. The feel of his lips, warm, soft, as they brushed hers. Those were the secret, naive imaginings of a girl who had never been courted, never been kissed. Fantasies.

But it was one thing to dream those things in her secret heart, in the dark of night while she lay in her cold, narrow bed. Quite another to be faced with the reality. Standing here in the dark little closet with Killian behind her was a far different thing.

Did he know? Could he tell that she had dreamed of him and watched him and fantasized about him for as long as she had been employed here at King's College? Foolish, girlish dreams, because he sought her opinion and listened to her words, because he laughed at her dry humor, because he was beautiful and intelligent and mysterious, and far more intriguing than any other man she had ever met.

Slowly, she turned, her heart pounding in anticipation, a wild, untrammeled rhythm, her mouth dry, her cheeks hot.

She saw now that he was not so close as she had anticipated, and she did not know if she was disappointed or relieved. He was standing in the alcove beyond the door, the insubstantial light that leaked down the narrow hallway from the main corridor leaving his features obscured by shadow.

"Miss Lowell," he greeted her, so polite, his tone low and smooth.

"Mr. Thayne." The words came out a cracked whisper, and she dropped her gaze to the tips of his polished boots. Always polished. His trousers always neat and pressed. His clothing impeccable and obviously expensive.

An oddity. Physicians to the upper class might earn quite a respectable income but a surgeon was less likely to do so and was definitely a rung below on the social ladder. All the more so a surgeon who practiced in a poor hospital such as King's College.

"Killian," he said.

She blinked, believing she had said his name aloud. Then she realized it was an invitation to use his given name. An inappropriate invitation.

"Mr. Thayne," she said, her tone inviting no further discussion. There was danger in even the slightest intimacy with this man. Speaking the syllables of his given name aloud would only heighten that danger.

Rolling her lips inward, she swiped her tongue across the surface, and waited, wondering what he was doing here. He had followed her. She could have no doubt of that, but the reason for such action escaped her.

"You defended me," he said. "I would like to know why."

He asked only why she defended him, not why she lied for him. The differentiation did not escape her.

Was there some import, some key relevance to his choice of words?

The shadows and his ever-present darkened spectacles masked his eyes and any secrets his expression might reveal.

"Does it matter?" she asked.

"You put yourself in a position of risk. That is...unacceptable," he said.

She wanted to laugh. She was in a position of risk more often than not. "Unacceptable to whom?"

"To me." His voice, low and rough wove through her.

"You have no right to feel that way," she whispered, hoping that her tone did not betray her, that he did not discern that part of her wanted him to have that right, the right of a friend...or lover.

"No, I do not." He looked away. "Why did you defend me?"

"I defended no one. I merely pointed out possible explanations for what had occurred and since no one came forth with any other, it appears my suggestion was given full merit." She paused. "Though I suspect this is not the end of the inquiry, nor the end of supposition and accusation."

His lips curved in a ghost of a smile, and she found herself staring at his mouth, the hard line of it, the slightly squared, full lower lip, so incredibly appealing. She could not seem to look away.

He had not shaved. His grooming was otherwise impeccable, but he eschewed the razor quite often. She wondered if there was a particular reason for that, or merely that he found it a bother.

There was no question that she liked it. Liked the look of his lean, squared jaw with the faintest hint of a cleft at the front of his chin. Of its own volition, her hand half rose, and she stopped the movement with a tiny gasp, wondering what she thought she had meant to do. Touch him? Lay her fingers against his jaw and feel the golden hairs beneath her fingers? She wondered if they would be soft or scratchy, and she could not suppress a small shiver.

"No, I suspect it is not the end of the inquiry," he agreed. He seemed not at all distressed by the observation.

Suddenly reckless, she dared ask, "Were you there this morning? Before I arrived? Was it you that I saw leaving Mr. Scully's bedside?"

His fine humor dropped away, and his expression turned cool and blank.

"What precisely did you see?" A harsh demand.

"I—" She backed up a step, put off by the sharp change in his tone, but the shelves were at her back and there was nowhere else for her to go.

He prowled a step closer. Her heart slammed hard against her ribs and she stared at him, afraid and appalled and tantalized all at once.

"Whom did you see, Miss Lowell?" He moderated his tone now, made it gentle and smooth. But he did not step back. He held his place, close enough that she had to tip her head far back to look into his eyes.

She liked it, liked his nearness, the scent of his skin, his size...and she thought that perhaps she oughtn't to like it. "Do you crowd me on purpose, sir?"

His teeth flashed white in a brief smile, and despite her words and tone, he made no move to step away. "And if I do?"

"Then I would ask you to explain such action. Do you intend it as a threat?"

He frowned. "No. Most assuredly not." He sounded appalled. "It seems I have forgotten the rules..." He took a step back, leaving a more decorous space between them.

"Rules?"

"Of polite discourse. Of flirta—" He broke off and scrubbed his palm over his jaw. "I am long out of practice."

"Polite discourse? We are in a supply closet talking about a dead man." Holding his gaze, she took a deliberate step forward, closing the gap. "Explain yourself."

He made no reply.

"You could have spoken with me in the ward or the corridor, yet you chose to follow me and engage in conversation here where we are alone. Why?" The words were a challenge, a demand, and she knew such confrontation was neither polite nor expected. But she was not one to act coy and cajole answers. She was only the person her father had raised her to be, the person she was inside, and she would not— could not—be other.

So she waited, arms crossed, head tipped.

"I like being close to you," he said with a rueful twist of his lips, his words warming her blood and leaving her dizzy. Dipping his head until his cheek brushed against her hair, he inhaled deeply. She stood very still, her pulse racing, her breath locked in her throat and all manner of strange and bright emotions cascading through her like a brook.

Only when he eased back did she dare to breathe, and even then, it was a short, huffing gasp. "You are inappropriate, sir."

He sighed. "I am." He took three steps back until he was at the far edge of the alcove. She regretted the loss of his proximity. His expression suggested he regretted the loss of hers. "Your hair smells like flowers," he said.

He left her breathless and warm and so aware of his assertion that it hummed in her blood. Her hair *did* smell like flowers. She bathed as often as possible using the scented soap that was her one excess, her baths her sole luxury, one she worked hard for, heating water and dragging it up the stairs to the hip bath she set up in her chamber. Mrs. Cowden and her fellow lodgers in Coptic Street thought her mad.

But this moment, with Killian Thayne noticing her in a way much the same as she noticed him, made her think that hours spent heating water and lugging buckets had been worth the effort.

Sarah closed her eyes, torn between the desire to stand here forever and the fact that anyone could come upon them.

As though he divined her thoughts, he said, "My apologies, Miss Lowell. Truly. I take liberties that are not mine to claim." And before she could form a response, he said, "Tell me what you saw this morning by Mr. Scully's bed."

"I am not certain." She was grateful for the change in topic and the tiny bit of space he allowed her. Her heart yet raced; her nerves tingled with excitement. He made her lose her common sense, and she did not like that. "Whatever I saw, it was not beside his bed, but rather on the far side of the ward. Perhaps I saw a shadow cast through the windows. Perhaps nothing." She paused and lifted her gaze, but found only her own reflection in the dark glass of his spectacles. "Perhaps I saw *you*."

"If you think that, then why did you defend me?" There was something in his tone that both pleased her and raised her hackles...affection? Amusement? He confounded her, made her wary, and yet, he fascinated her.

"I never said I thought it. You asked what I saw, and as I truly do not know, I offered a variety of options. I cannot say why I leaped to your defense." She only knew that she could not find it in herself to believe that he had ripped open the wrists of four patients at King's College and drained their bodies of blood.

Even standing here in the gloomy little closet with the height and breadth of him—the *threat* of him—blocking her path, the possibility that he had done murder seemed absurd. She had seen him work far too hard to save patients' lives to believe that he would choose to rob them of it.

He reached up and slid his spectacles down his nose, then dragged them off entirely, leaving his gaze open to her scrutiny. The shadows only served to accent the handsome lines and planes of his features. The slash of high cheekbones, the straight line of his nose.

For a long moment, he studied her, saying nothing, the only sound the escalated cadence of her own breathing. He was so focused, so intent.

Again, she wondered if he was a mesmerist, for she found she could not look away. Had no wish to look away.

Her limbs felt heavy, languid, and her blood was thick and hot in her veins.

He moved aside and swept his hand before him, offering her the opportunity to exit the closet. She hesitated then shook her head and stayed where she was.

"No?" he asked and waited.

Again, she shook her head, knowing it was folly, yet unwilling to simply walk away from this moment. She held his gaze as he stepped inside the closet once more, held it as he moved closer and then closer still, held it as he raised his hand and laid his fingers along the side of her throat where her pulse pounded hard and wild.

"Sarah." Just her name, spoken in his low, deep voice. The sound thrummed through her body, leaving her limbs trembling and her thoughts befuddled. "Such a wise and brave treasure you are."

Wise. Brave. Was she? Or was she a fool, making choices that were ill advised, even dangerous?

Treasure.

He rested the back of his hand against her cheek and she fought the urge to lean into his touch. How long since she had been touched with affection? Months and months. And even then, not like this. Never like this.

"I believe that in a different time, you would make a fine physician and surgeon," he said, his voice rougher than she had ever heard it. "Dr. Sarah Lowell has a pleasant ring."

She cut him a glance through her lashes. "Your words are fantastical. No medical school would offer a place to a woman."

"And if they did?"

He laid bare a secret dream, one she had shared with no one, not even her father. She *would* make a fine surgeon. She knew she would. But such was not to be.

"If wishes were fishes..." She made a soft laugh.

"...we'd all swim in riches." Killian smiled at her. "I like the sound of your laughter," he said.

Her skin tingled, her nerves danced, and she was aware of his every breath, of the sweep of his dark gold lashes, the line of his brow, the shape of his lips.

A sound escaped her, a breath, a sigh. He leaned closer until their breath mingled. She wanted to rest her nose against the strong column of his throat and simply breathe him in, but she held her place, paralyzed by incertitude and inexperience.

He would kiss her now. She wanted him to kiss her now.

Her lips parted.

Voices carried to them from the main corridor, laughter and the murmur of conversation. The moment dropped and shattered, fractured into a thousand bits. Sarah felt the loss like a physical blow.

With a rueful smile, Killian drew his knuckles along the curve of her cheek, making her shiver. Then he dropped his hand and stepped away, leaving her body aching in the strangest way, as though her breasts and belly were pained by disappointment.

She closed her eyes, drew a deep breath, and when she opened them once more, he was gone and she was alone. Alone with the shadows and the dark and the memory of the way he had looked at her, his features hard and lean with...hunger.

Only when she turned and reached for the supplies that she had set on the shelf did she see a brilliant white handkerchief atop the pile, the four corners drawn together and tied in a knot.

"How...?" Somehow, Killian had put this here without her noticing. She untied the knot and the corners fell away, revealing an elaborate "T" embroidered in one corner, the pristine linen stained by grease from a golden pasty neatly aligned in the center of the square, the edges of the dough crimped, the scent of meat and pepper and potato tickling her senses.

She broke off a corner and popped it in her mouth, the flavors bursting on her tongue. She ate the whole pasty, one delicious bite at a time, and then folded the handkerchief, knowing she ought to return it.

Knowing she would keep it.

8

Killian knew she was an innocent. Not in the sense that she lacked knowledge. He had every confidence that Sarah Lowell knew a great deal about both male and female anatomy and how the two fit together. But such knowledge did not equate to experience, and there she lacked.

The beast at his core stirred, pleased that she had lain with no man. *Mine.*

The thought was not in his nature.

It is. You are a beast driven by appetites. It is in your nature to claim what you want.

Then he would defy his nature.

But there in the dim closet with the shadows playing across her skin and her lips ripe and moist, he had been hard pressed to keep his distance. Her straight, dark hair had been pinned at her nape, begging to be set free to tumble over her shoulders. He'd wanted to peel the clothes off her body and leave her only her unbound hair for adornment.

She was not beautiful by conventional standards, but he had no use for such standards. They changed with each passing decade and he had watched them come and go. To him, Sarah Lowell was more than beautiful. Her nose was small, her lips ripe, her chin stubborn. And each time he looked at her, he saw something new and wonderful. A small freckle at the corner of her lip. A slight imbalance between her right and left brow that made her face unique, expressive...perfect.

The scent of her skin intoxicated him.

The sweep of her lashes enthralled him.

He wanted her with an intensity that made no sense. He wanted to pin her beneath him, take her, conquer her, mark her as his. He wanted her body. He wanted her blood, not to feed, but to bind her to him. He wanted her not merely because she was soft and smelled like flowers or because her curves were apparent and lush beneath the ugly dresses she wore or because her gaze held his without guile. He wanted her because he *liked* her, because he enjoyed their conversation, because he anticipated the soft huff of her laughter...and that was a danger.

It had taken iron will to touch her cheek and step away, to leave her there in the closet aching for his touch.

That was the worst of it. The knowledge that she wanted him. The knowledge that she would welcome him.

He had no right.

❧ 9 ❧

Sarah came to work before dawn each day and walked home each night long past dusk. The sun she saw only through the grimy windows of the wards or the corridors.

She had grown wily, careful to vary her route between her room in Coptic Street and the hospital, but every route skirted the dangerous edges of St. Giles. Twice more, she had seen a man standing by the gravestones, watching her as she entered the hospital. Not just a silhouette or a man-shaped shadow. *A man.* There could be no doubt now. He never approached her, never made any truly menacing move, but he was there, always there, and his presence unnerved her.

Yesterday, she had dared to turn in his direction and take a step toward him, intending to call out to him from across the way. Her attention had forced him deeper into the gloom. Clearly, he had no wish to entertain her company, only to watch her from a distance.

A menacing conundrum.

Now, Sarah turned her attention to Elinor, who stood by her side holding a stack of clean bandages to replace the blood and pus-stained cloths that Sarah had just unwound from a dressed wound. The patient was stoic, lips pressed together in a tight line, eyes dull with pain.

"You're adept at that," Elinor said. "As good as any of the sisters. As good as any of the attendants. Better, I think." She glanced around. "But you take a risk. I think you oughtn't. Last time—" She broke off and sighed.

Last time the matron had discovered that Sarah had tended a wound, she had lectured her about overstepping her place and Sarah had waited for the woman to dismiss her. Sarah had cautioned the patient not to divulge the fact that it was she who had removed cloth and stones and stitched the gash shut. He had not heeded her request. That the patient had recovered did nothing to sway judgment in Sarah's favor. It had been only the arrival of Mr. Thayne who insisted he had been the one to treat the wound and Sarah had merely been a bystander that had saved her. He said the patient had been out of his head and confused. Matron had relented, but her warning to Sarah against further transgression had been stern.

When Sarah had tried to broach the matter with Mr. Thayne, he had only shaken his head and said, "Do you think I am as adept with a needle as the fellow's wife?"

Sarah knew then that Mr. Thayne had observed her that night and chosen to stay silent. Never one to look a gift horse in the mouth, she had shrugged and replied, "Perhaps."

"This time is different," Sarah said now to Elinor. "Two of the sisters are sick with the ague, and one apprentice as well. The surgeons are occupied elsewhere." She accepted another bandage from Elinor. "Which means that I have been tasked with doing whatever needs to be done." She shrugged. "This needs to be done."

"And you'll do a better job than the lot of them," Elinor said with a nod, her gathered curls bouncing. She leaned in to get a better look at Sarah's handiwork. "Why bandage the wound in fresh cloth? Why not just wipe it like the surgeons do and rewrap it? Or leave it alone? Mr. Franks says it is best not to disturb a healing wound."

"Almost done," Sarah said to the patient, who offered a nod and a wan smile. Then she answered Elinor without looking up, her movements deft and sure as she tied off the bandage. "I do as my father did. He believed it necessary to unwrap and examine the wound. And he never set a used dressing back in place. He said the foul humors would result in putrefaction."

"Did he?" Elinor sounded interested rather than dubious.

The sounds of footsteps carried from the hallway. Sarah glanced at the open door. One of the apprentices hurried past, and she looked away, disappointed. She had seen Mr. Thayne—Killian—only in passing since their exchange in the closet. But she had found an orange on the stool beneath her cloak four days past, and yesterday, he'd left a ham sandwich. He seemed determined to feed her. And he somehow divined her favorites.

Raising her head, she found Elinor watching her with a knowing gaze, one tinged with concern.

"I saw one of the apprentices watching you," she said. "He's young and sweet. Pleasant face. Clean fingernails. I could point him out if you like."

Sarah huffed a short laugh. "I think not. Though clean fingernails do much to recommend him."

Elinor shook her head. "Don't be soured on men just because I am. They aren't all like my lump of a husband."

"I know that. I just..." Sarah shrugged. "A young and sweet apprentice does not interest me."

Elinor sighed. "You've set your sights on him and no other will do." She caught Sarah's wrist and Sarah glanced at her, reading all the worry and distress in her friend's expression. "Mr. Thayne is neither simple nor sweet, Sarah. He is young and handsome. I'll give him that. But his soul is old. And there is something..." She shook her head. "Something *other* about him. Something distant and dangerous."

Sarah opened her mouth. Closed it. Finally, she said, "I have not set my sights on anyone." *Liar.*

She moved to the next bed, the next patient who lay snoring. Elinor followed and with a quick glance about, lowered her voice and said, "I passed Mrs. McKeever on her way out as I was coming in this morning and she said that some believe Mr. Thayne killed all four of the dead patients in a mad fit."

The words came as no surprise. The entire hospital had been buzzing with conjecture and whispered supposition for days. Some thought an animal with a burrow in the walls had killed all four. Some thought a creature of the night stole through the darkened corridors.

There was all manner of conjectures as to the culprit. One thing she knew: no one who was a patient of Mr. Thayne's had a bad word to say about him.

A mad fit. She had never seen Killian less than composed and controlled...except for a single moment in the closet when she had thought he might kiss her. There had been a tiny fracture in his control then.

"Mr. Thayne is an extremely competent surgeon," Sarah replied as she unwound the dressing from the patient's arm. The woman stirred and mumbled a protest but did not wake.

Elinor made a sound of displeasure. "He is. That fact is not in question."

Sarah cut her a sidelong glance. "And you, Elinor? Do you believe the gossip?"

Elinor searched her face. "I believe people gossip too much. Including me." She lowered her voice once more. "A constable was here yesterday. From the Metropolitan Police."

Sarah murmured a wordless reply, for she already knew of the constable's visit, having heard about it not only from the night nurse, but one of the lads who brought the morning gruel, the laundress, and two of the apothecary apprentices.

"The constable spoke with Mr. Simon and Mr. Franks, and after that with Mr. Thayne, but in the end, he left. I thought he might like tea, so I went after him and asked about that."

"Of course you did," Sarah said.

"I'm nothing if not hospitable." Elinor smiled, dimples in her cheeks.

"And inquisitive. Out with it, then. What did he say?"

Elinor shook her head. "He very politely declined the tea, saying he found the place off-putting."

"I can't imagine why..." Sarah swabbed the wound, pleased to see the healthy pink of newly healed skin and no sign of infection.

Elinor snorted. "He did share enough conversation that I can tell you he was called in to investigate by Mr. Simon, and that he will not be back." She unfolded another bandage and handed it to Sarah. "It seems that the constable holds the opinion that people die in hospitals, and without further evidence, he cannot think there is foul play afoot."

Something in her tone made Sarah pause in her work and turn her head to offer her full attention.

Elinor tapped her foot on the wooden floor, a rapid patter. She pursed her lips, and after a moment continued in a whisper. "But I wonder. I do. I worked at Guy's Hospital before I came here, and I've never seen the like of those wounds, ripped open and not a drop of blood shed."

Sarah stared at her for a long moment, having no words, but so many thoughts. Because she, too, wondered, not just about the wound, but about the shadow she had seen the morning Mr. Scully died, and about Killian Thayne's presence beside the bed of the woman who had died two weeks before that. She was certain that he was not responsible, a certainty that dwelled in instinct rather than quantifiable fact. But was such faith in him folly?

Wetting her lips, she shook her head. "We need more bandages, Elinor," she said, her voice soft, her heart heavy. She did not want to wonder about him. She wanted to believe that he was exactly the man she conjured in her dreams.

The trouble was, she had learned both in the months leading up to her father's death and the months since then that the boundary between dreams and nightmares was wont to blur.

SARAH DREW HER CLOAK TIGHT ABOUT HER SHOULDERS. THE NIGHT was cold and clear, the stars winking bright and pretty against the dark blue-black sky, a sliver of moon offering pale light. Her gaze strayed to the graveyard. There was nothing there save old stones and a single ancient tree, its gnarled branches casting creeping shadows along the ground.

Still, she shivered, in part from the chill, and in part from the certainty that he would come, the man who watched her. He would follow her through the wretched, twisted streets and alleys of St. Giles.

He would not approach. He would walk close enough that she

would know he was there, but not close enough for her to see him. The pattern was set.

She hated it. Hated the feeling of impotency and the ever-present fear that this time he would break the pattern, draw near, reveal his dark intent.

The wind howled down from the north, pushing up under her cloak, chilling her to the bone. The temptation to take the shortest route was strong, for it halved the distance and would bring her to Coptic Street that much faster. But that route was the least safe of her choices, and so she would take the longer and hope that the crowds kept the man who stalked her away.

She began to walk, her cudgel gripped in her fist beneath the material of her cloak. Her steps were quick and sure, her senses alert. She heard nothing, felt no creeping certainty that she was being watched, but the streets were far from safe and she was yet far from home.

Home. Such a strange word to apply to the tiny, cramped room where she slept each night. She had grown up in a pretty house with fine china and a pot of chocolate every morning. They had employed a cook, a maid-of-all-work, and her father's man who was valet, coachman, butler, and footman all rolled into one. They had not been wealthy, but they had made do quite nicely, she and her father, a physician who saw mostly to the health needs of merchants and tradesmen. Not the upper class, but not the poor, which meant her father had always been paid moderately well.

She had never expected her pleasant life to be anything else.

But then, inexplicably, her father's temperament had changed, his mood fraying, his thoughts and actions growing irrational. After months of steady decline and frightening and unusual behavior, he died. He was alive one night and dead the next morning, fallen in the Thames, his body never found. The only reason that Sarah knew anything of his fate was because he had been accompanied that night by an old friend, Dr. Grammercy, who had tried to find him and fish him out of the river, to no avail. It was a terrible and tragic culmination of months of descent into what she suspected was opium addiction.

With his death, Sarah had found herself without funds, evicted from her home. She could not say precisely how that had happened.

She had never thought her father the type to squander his money, but in the months before his death, he had spent it on something that defied her understanding.

A cure, he had insisted. He was searching for a cure.

She could have told him that the only cure was to stop taking the drug. She thought now that she *should* have told him that.

Well, it mattered little, she thought now as she passed the small cramped houses that backed onto the slaughterhouses, the smell of death and old blood always heavy in the air. Come morning, there would be children running in the street next to a herd of pigs, with inches of blood flowing beneath their feet. A terrible place, really.

She kept her head down as she hurried past. It was too late to change what her father had done, what he had become—an opium addict. She must only find a way to go on.

Turning onto Queen Street, she was confronted by light from the street lamps and sound and a tight press of bodies that she navigated with care. Near Drury Lane, the public houses spilled their patrons into the streets. To her left, two men engaged in fisticuffs, dancing about to the taunts and calls of their fellows. To her right, three women were screaming like harpies, pulling and yanking on an old dress stretched out between them, none of them willing to relinquish their grasp.

The next street was narrower, with fewer people, and the street after that narrower and less crowded still. Now her route brought her to a place where she could no longer avoid the dimness and the shadows. There was only one lamp on the road, and tonight it was unlit. She quickened her pace and ducked down an alley.

A staircase ascended the outside of the building and a man, bowed and bent, slogged up the steps, a sack of cabbages slung over his back. He would peel the outer leaves off on the morrow and take them to sell as fresh, though they were likely already several days old. It was a trick she had never suspected before her life had brought her to St. Giles.

Sarah scanned the shadows and moved on, unease trickling through her now. This was the part of her trek she liked the least.

Again, she turned, this time into an alley narrower than the last.

Almost there. Her boots rang on the cobbled pavement, her heart pounded a wild rhythm.

She walked very quickly now, the wind tunneling down the alley to sting her eyes, her cheeks, and behind her, she heard footsteps. Not ringing like her own. Shuffling, sliding.

He was there, behind her. She could *hear* him.

Her breath came in ragged rasps and she dragged her cudgel free of the draping material of her cloak, holding it before her at the ready as she quickened her pace even more.

There was nowhere safe, nowhere she could turn.

The courtyards that fed off the narrow alley held their own dangers, for she knew not what manner of men, or women, might lurk there. In this place, poverty forced even women and children to toss aside morals and do what they must to survive. Calling out for help was therefore not an attractive option.

Ahead of her loomed a dark shape, and she skidded to a stop, horrified to realize that a large wooden cart blocked her path.

From behind her came the sound of cloth flapping in the wind, and she whirled about, her cudgel raised and ready.

The light here was so dim, there was only charcoal shadow painted on shadow, but she knew what she saw. The shape of a man loomed some twenty feet away. He was draped in a dark cloak that lifted and fanned out in the wind like the wings of a raven. His features were completely obscured by a low crowned hat pulled down over his brow.

He was tall and broad and menacing...familiar somehow, his height and the shape of his shadow...similar to the shadow she thought she had seen on the ward the morning Mr. Scully died. But it was more than that...something else familiar...

Trembling, she clenched her teeth to keep them from clacking aloud. If she dared cry for help, she might bring down a dozen worse creatures on her head.

Taking a step backward, and another, she pressed against the wood of the cart, her legs shaking so hard, she knew not how they yet bore her weight.

Run, her mind screamed, and she dared a rapid glance in each direction. To her right was a courtyard, to her left, another alley.

The man before her took a single step forward, menacing. Terrifying. He was done toying with her. He was coming for her, as she had always known he would.

Still clutching her cudgel, she snaked her free hand behind her back and groped for the wooden cart. It was high-wheeled, and she could feel the lower limit of it at a level with her waist.

There was her best choice.

She dropped to the ground and rolled beneath the cart.

Her pursuer made a sound of surprise. For the briefest instant, she wasn't certain if it was a hiss, or her name—*Ssssarah*—but she did not pause to look behind her. Bounding to her feet as soon as she reached the opposite side of the cart, she grabbed her skirt with her free hand and hauled it up, then ran as fast as she could, her legs pumping, her breath rasping in her throat.

The cobbles were caked with years of grime and refuse, and her feet skidded and slipped on the sludge. Once, she slammed her shoulder against a wall, nearly falling, but she pushed herself upright and ran on, weaving through the alleys, taking any turn she recognized, not daring to take those that were less than familiar.

The only thing worse than being chased through this warren would be running blindly without having a clear concept of her location.

Twice, she dared look behind her. She saw nothing to make her think she had been followed.

Finally, she ducked into a shadowed niche beneath a narrow wooden stairwell. Her lungs screamed for air, and she huddled as deep in the gloom as she could, pulling her body in tight to make herself as small as possible. Her ears strained to hear the sound of footsteps pounding in pursuit, but there was nothing.

From the window above her came the discordant noise of an argument, a man's voice, then another, deeper voice in reply, and a moment later, the dull thud of fists on flesh and a cry of pain.

Panting, she struggled to satisfy her desperate need for air and will her galloping pulse to a more sedate pace.

She waited a moment longer then crept from her hiding place. Staying close to the wall and the sheltering gloom, she made her way clear of the labyrinth of alleys to New Oxford Street. There she crossed and then continued north to the small lodging house where she rented her room from Mrs. Cowden.

She strode along the street toward the narrow house hemmed in on both sides by other narrow houses. Almost had she reached the place when she drew up short and stumbled to a dead stop. Fear lodged in her throat like a fishbone. Just ahead, a man lounged against the light post several houses away.

A tall man, garbed in a long, dark cloak.

The wind caught the cloak and made it billow like a sail. Sarah stood rooted to the spot, uncertain whether to run for the door of her lodging house or flee down the empty street.

He stood on the far side of the lamp-post his face obscured. Then he shifted, and the light from the lamp spilled down, glinting off the metal rims of his spectacles and highlighting the sun bright hair that framed his angular face.

❧ 10 ❧

Barcelona, Spain, 1585

THE INQUISITOR'S CHAMBER HAD WALLS OF STONE WITH TWO BARRED *windows set close to the high ceiling. Darkened hallways branched off the main room like the legs of a spider. Killian stayed close to Layla's side. She trembled, from fear or cold or anticipation he could not say.*

He almost turned back, almost drew her from this place of pain and torment, but he stifled the inclination and drew her forward instead. He refused to carry out the task he had set himself without her full and clear consent. He had brought her here so she could see the truth of what he was, what she would become.

He had met her by happenstance, a dying woman who desperately wanted to live. She was the sister of a man with whom he carried out business. He did not love her—was one such as he even capable of love?—and she did not love him. Theirs was a friendship of mutual respect and companionship. She was intelligent and shrewd, and their conversation was amusing. After months of watching her slowly fade away, he had told her he could offer a cure, he could save her life.

The offer was made not only for her sake but for his. He was weary of his solitude. The lovers he had taken over the years had been fleeting distractions, women who were well aware that he would never be a permanent fixture in their lives. He had told none what he was, shared little of himself with any of them. But Layla was not a bedmate. She was a friend, and he thought that was a good basis for the solution he offered: a way to cheat her rapidly approaching death.

He had shared few details, had only warned that she would have to do things that were both distasteful and against her nature in order to survive.

"I do not care," she had said, her dark eyes flashing in her pale face. "I want to live, whatever the cost, I want to live." She had paused. "Do you do those distasteful things?"

"I do. Do not misunderstand. I do not revile what I have become." What his mother's murderer had made him. "It simply is. And because of it, I have had opportunities to travel, to study, to see wonders others can only imagine. Pyramids. Tigers. Monkeys in a jungle thick and green. Rome, Venice, Paris, London..."

And always he moved on after a few short years, never offering the chance for any to notice that he never aged, never grew ill. Never allowing himself the opportunity for friendships or connections of much length or depth. It was a lonely existence, one he had lived for over two centuries. In his human life, he had enjoyed interludes of quiet and equal interludes of camaraderie. But he was no longer human, and whatever interactions he shared with mortals could never be enough to breach the walls between them for he was the hunter and they were his prey.

In the beginning, there had been occasions when he had considered walking into the sun. But he had not, for his yearning to live, to learn, to feed off experiences, and yes, to help mankind and atone in some tiny way for the lives he stole had outweighed his melancholy. The plague that had killed his family—that he had brought to his family—had sparked in him a need to understand disease and death, to bring ease to the suffering of others, to find cures where he could. So he studied texts and healed those he could; those he could not heal, those who were already wrapped in death's embrace but had yet to draw their last breath, he drained.

Layla looked up at him now in the dim light, her face pale, her dark hair tumbling over her shoulders.

"For everything you gain from this choice, there will be sacrifice in equal measure," he warned.

He had not made this offer before. He was not even certain he could succeed in her transformation for his plan of action was based solely on the hazy recollections of his own rushed and terrifying transition. She might die during the process. She would definitely die without it.

She nodded.

"Come." He offered his arm and she took it, leaning heavily upon him as they moved from the Inquisitor's chamber to a narrow hallway with small cells on either side. When they reached the end of the corridor, Killian stopped. He held to the shadows, his form draped all in black, invisible to the wretch who lay on the ground where he had been tossed.

Killian had come to this place because he had heard this man's cries and pleas.

He was doomed, this man who was a husband and father, whose crime was labeled heresy because he refused to forsake his religion and replace it with another. He had been accused and detained. Tortured. Tried. Sentenced.

Killian had not been there to witness the man's torment. But he knew what had been done because he knew the human body and could read the signs in the prisoner's broken and bloodied form.

Beside him, Layla's every breath was too fast, too shallow. He could hear her pulse, the racing of her heart, the pounding of the blood in her veins. Sweet blood, hot and alive. After this night, her blood, her heart, her very physiology would be permanently altered.

It was an easy matter for Killian to enter the cell, to hunker down by the prisoner's side, to ask him, "Why do you beg to die? I heard you as I passed by, calling out for a merciful death."

The man's lips were dry and cracked and it took him a moment to manage a reply. "Are you an apparition?"

"I am not." Killian rested his hand on the man's injured shoulder and held his gaze, willing him to feel no pain, no fear. He supposed this ability to lull mortals into a state of calm repose was a handy thing when his survival required him to kill them. A calm victim was far easier to drain than one who struggled. And for the victim, it was far easier to die without fear. "Tell me why you wish to die."

"They will burn me at the stake on the morrow," the prisoner said, his words *even and soft now.* "*They have denied me death by garrote before burning. They will burn me alive.*" *He closed his eyes.* "*Kill me quickly. Kill me now. Deny them their pyre. Show me mercy.*"

Layla made a low moan, and Killian looked up to find that she had moved to the door of the small cell. "*Hurry,*" *she said.* "*Bring him and let us be away.*"

"*You think I brought you here to save this man from his fate?*" *Killian asked.* "*After my warnings and admonitions, you believe I brought you here for that?*"

Layla wrapped her arms around herself, resting her shoulder heavily on the bars. Her eyes were liquid, the shadows and dim light making them larger and darker, like the hollowed sockets of a skeletal skull.

Killian shook his head. "*I brought you here to watch me feed, to understand what fate you beg for. I told you that your life would be purchased with compromises, with the need to do things. Disturbing things.*"

"*Feed?*" *she whispered with a glance at the broken man who lay on the floor.*

"*I am here to kill him,*" *Killian said.* "*A kindness, in truth. Mercy.*" *He said the last though he was not certain there was such a thing as a merciful monster.*

"*A kindness?*" *Layla took a step back, horror etching her features.*

"*Death at my hand will be swift and painless.*"

"*We can take him from this place. We can save him,*" *Layla said, but the words wavered and dipped, as though she already accepted that she argued against the inevitable.*

Killian made a gesture to encompass the cell and the hallway beyond. "*I cannot save them all.*" *He had learned that long ago. He had learned that humans would die and he would not. He had learned not to let his hunger grow to the point that he fed indiscriminately, a feral creature driven by need. He had learned to kill those who were evil or those on the brink of death. His conscience sat better on his shoulders that way. This kill was a mercy.*

"*Watch now,*" *he said.* "*Learn. You will need these skills.*"

She sank to her knees on the cold stone, as though his words stole the last of her strength. "*What are you?*" *she whispered.*

He had not expected it, her horror and revulsion. But he saw now that he should have. He thought back to the human boy-man he had been before the stranger came to his family's home. He had not been offered a choice between death and monster. The monster had bred a monster and then walked out to burn in the sun.

Would Kjell have chosen life if the creature had let him choose?

Killian did not know. He was Kjell no longer, and he had not been human in a very long while. He was Killian now, and Killian needed to feed.

A warning of the coming dawn crawled across his skin; it was less than an hour away. If he tarried here any longer, the dawn would flay his skin and burn hotter than the pyre this wretch feared. He needed to finish here and seek the darkness.

He lifted the man's head to his lap. He pulled his knife free. He no longer gnawed open a vein to feed. He was a civilized monster, one that made use of a utensil. With a deft slash, he severed the carotid artery in the man's throat and sealed his lips to the wound as the blood spurted free. And he fed.

When he was done, he wiped the blood from his lips and went to kneel by Layla's side. She flinched away.

She cried out in protest as he lifted her in his arms, she was light but his heart was heavy. He had miscalculated and he suspected that this foray would not end as he had planned. He carried her to her home, to her bed, and when he set her down he asked, "Do you want to live?"

"Not like that. Not like you." She scrabbled back, as far from him as she could. But he expected that. She had held herself stiff in his arms, trembling and sobbing the entire way home.

"Where is the woman who said, 'I want to live, whatever the cost, I want to live'?"

She came up on her knees, her hair tumbling over her shoulders, her skin white, traced with blue veins, her eyes burning and wild. "She would rather die than be like you. You are a monster."

"I am." A foolish monster who had dared hope he could create a monstrous companion.

She looked at him now with only terror and revulsion. Gone was the clever wit and laughter.

Gone was his hope.

"Get out. Go!"

He went without looking back.

She died not long after. He was not there for her passing or her burial. But he had paid a man to report back and so he knew that she had not been alone, for she had a brother who loved her as Kjell had loved his sisters so very long ago.

Killian was glad she had not been alone.

Sarah stared at Killian where he stood under the street lamp. Had he followed her? Had he been the one stalking her—hunting her—in the dim alleys?

Her pursuer had been behind her, yet Killian had arrived here before her, an unlikely outcome if he was the man who had chased her —unless he had taken to the skies and flown like a bat. His breathing was slow and even while her lungs sucked in great gasps of air, her heart pounding a frantic rhythm thanks to her flight through the poorly lit streets.

"What are you doing here?" The question she had meant to speak in ringing tones came out shaky and weak. "What are you doing here?" she asked again, strident now, her breath blowing white before her lips.

His brows drew down as he straightened, lifting his shoulder from the post.

"Do not come closer," she said, holding her cudgel before her.

He stilled. His head was uncovered. Her gaze dropped to his hands, searching for a low-crowned hat like the one her pursuer had worn. But his hands were empty, his skin bare. He did not wear gloves, though the wind was bitter. Her pursuer had worn gloves; she was certain of it.

"Do you have a hat? Gloves?" she demanded.

"Sarah," he said, his brow furrowed in concern as he took a step toward her. Not Miss Lowell. *Sarah.* The way he said her name in his warm-chocolate voice made her heart twitch.

She held up one hand, palm forward. Again, he stilled. "Do you?" she asked.

"No. I have neither hat nor gloves."

She exhaled, forcing her shoulders down, unclenching her fists. She studied his face and her emotions danced from fear to elation. Because Killian was here, waiting for her, staring down at her with unwavering intensity.

Then anger crashed in a wave, dampening her terror and panic and unreasoning joy. Anger at Killian, though she could not say why. Anger at the man who stalked her. Anger at herself, at her circumstance, at the way her heart lifted simply because Killian was here.

She did not know herself in that instant. She was not this girl.

"What is it?" he asked, lifting one hand as though reaching for hers, then dropping it back to his side before he made contact. She yearned for that contact even as she drew back to avoid it.

"I was—" she glanced over her shoulder, almost expecting a second man to materialize behind her, one with black gloves and a black hat. When she saw no one there, she turned to face him once more "—followed. Someone followed me from King's College. A man. Tall. Garbed in black. He wore a low crowned hat. He chased me through St. Giles."

"Chased you?" Killian's gaze flicked along the empty street and something in his expression gave her pause. She glanced back, but the street behind her was empty.

"It was not the first time," Sarah said. "He follows me all the time but this is the first he has come so close. He knew my name. He said my name. At least...I think it was my name." She pressed her lips together, stilling the flow of words.

Again, Killian looked to the street. She followed his gaze. The night was dark, save for the twinkling stars and a thin sliver of moon. The shadows were darker still. Only the one lamp shone, casting its glow in a circle some ten feet across, then fading away to nothing at the periphery.

Yet Killian perused the dark street as though he could see things that were veiled from her sight.

"He is not there now," he said. From a distance, a faded cacophony of laughter and shrieks carried to them through the cold air.

"But he was. Has been. In the mornings. At night. He is always there. My shadow." She did not doubt her own perception of that.

Killian tipped his head toward her. "I believe you."

His simple assertion summoned a flood of relief, vindication, though it should not matter if he believed her or not. Nonplussed, she waved a hand toward his dark spectacles. "I cannot imagine that you can discern anything wearing those. The street is dark as Hades, and your spectacles make it more so."

"I see as well with them as without. Better, in fact." He offered a one-shouldered shrug, the casual gesture out of keeping with his normally reserved manner. "My eyes are sensitive to light."

She stared at him, thinking his comment a jest. But his expression showed him to be in earnest. "But it is night. There is little light."

"I see what others do not." He studied the street a moment longer, and then he turned toward her and smiled. Despite everything—her breathless run, her fear, her disorientation—that smile touched a place inside her, making it crackle and flare like a spark roused to flame.

"Hades," he said.

"I beg your pardon?"

"You said the street is dark as Hades. Do you refer to the Greek god of the Underworld or the shadowy place itself?"

She blinked. "The place."

Killian clasped his hands behind his back and tipped his face to the sky. "How do you know Hades is dark? I always imagined it belching tongues of fire which would make it quite bright, I should think."

"You are attempting to distract me from my distress."

"I am. And I appear to be doing a poor job of it."

His gaze dropped to her hands, and she realized then that she was turning the thick stick she carried over and over in nervous inattention. He eased it from her cold and numbed fingers, then tested the weight of it on his open palm.

"Why not a pistol?" he asked.

"You do not seem surprised to discover that I carry a weapon."

"I am not surprised. You are a most intelligent and resourceful woman, Miss Lowell."

He thought her intelligent, resourceful. She found his words more appealing than any poetic praise of her eyes or lips or hair.

He handed the stick back to her, and she sucked in a breath as their fingers touched, hers gloved, his bare. Even through the wool of her gloves, she felt the warmth of his skin. She frowned, stared at his naked hands. They should be cold, not warm.

"So why not a pistol?" he prodded.

"I would need to learn to shoot it with accuracy, and such knowledge comes only with a great deal of practice," she said. "Besides, pistols are costly."

"Why not a knife, then?" he asked.

She could see that he asked the question out of genuine interest, that he expected a reply.

"I am small. My assailant might be large. It would be too easy for him to twist a knife from my hand and turn it upon me. Besides, carrying a knife is more complicated. I would need some sort of sheath to protect me from the blade. And then there is the cost of acquiring both knife and sheath..."

His straight brows rose above the limits of his spectacles. "But you feel confident to wield your stick?"

"Cudgel," she said. "Confident enough. No one would expect me to have it, and I have a good chance at landing a solid blow to the underside of a man's chin or his privates or across his shins or kneecaps before an attacker could know my intent."

"Wise and brave," he murmured.

She pressed her lips together, disconcerted by his praise.

"And how did you learn to wield your cudgel well?" he asked.

"Perhaps I do not wield it well," Sarah said.

"Perhaps. But the way you hold it suggests otherwise."

"Do you know a great deal about cudgels?" she asked.

"Less than you, I suspect." His smile widened to a grin, white teeth and a dimple in his cheek. "Who taught you?"

His smile lured her to smile back, even as she wondered at this odd conversation they were having in the middle of Coptic Street on a sharp, frigid night.

"My landlady. She stuffed a sack with rags and made me hit it until she was satisfied."

"I see. A formidable woman, your landlady?"

Sarah thought of Mrs. Cowden who was shorter than Sarah by several inches, who had survived the deaths of three children and her husband, who rented rooms to those in need, who taught a naïve young woman how to protect herself, and she said, "Formidable, indeed." She paused then asked again, "What are you doing here?"

"Waiting. For you."

"Why?" Sarah stared at him. "And how did you know where to find me?"

The wind picked up, snatching at her cloak, her hair, making her shiver. Killian took note of that and glanced about, his attention turning to the lodging house.

"You are cold. Perhaps we might take this conversation inside to the parlor. You will be more comfortable."

She noticed that he made no mention of his own discomfort in the chilly night.

"The parlor?" She laughed at that. Oh, that he thought she lived in such a fine place—the expectation of a parlor—was both funny and sad. "On the ground floor are the kitchen and the dining room and the landlady's rooms. The first and second floors are all to let. There is no parlor."

Reaching up, he drew off his spectacles, and she was struck again by the beauty of his eyes, silvery gray against the thick sweep of dark gold lashes.

"Then we may take this conversation to the room you rent."

"I take a very small room from Mrs. Cowden," she demurred, struck by the image of him, tall and masculine, filling the tiny space of her chamber. Standing beside her narrow bed. The thought made her breath catch because he had been there before, many times over, but only in her dreams and imaginings. To have him there in truth would be both daunting and alluring. "There is not even a sitting room. I cannot have you come in at this hour of the night, Mr. Thayne."

"Killian," he murmured absently, his gaze sliding to the front of the house. The brick was dirty and the yard ill kept. Mrs. Cowden was anything but house proud, her fondness for gin overtaking her fondness for anything else. Sarah felt absurdly unveiled to have him study the house with such careful regard. "You must call me Killian."

Killian. She dared not say his name aloud, lest he read her secret longings in the way her lips shaped and caressed the syllables.

"I am going inside now, where it is warm—" an untruth, for though it would be sweltering hot next to the kitchen fire, the remainder of the house was bound to be little warmer than the brutal climes she was subject to outdoors "—and where I hope Mrs. Cowden has kept a plate for me. Whatever you wished to discuss will have to wait for the morrow. At the hospital." She frowned. "How *did* you find me?"

Again, he looked to the street, his gaze alert. The focused intensity of his perusal was enough to stoke the embers of her unease. She tried to see what he saw but could make out only the shapes of the neighboring houses.

"Does it matter?" he asked without looking at her. "I am here now."

"Yes. It matters."

He glanced at her then returned his attention to the road. "Matron keeps a written record."

She almost expressed her surprise that the matron had shared such information. Then she realized he had not said she had. He had only said she kept a record. Had Killian searched the matron's office without her knowledge? He wouldn't dare.

Oh, but he would.

Killian's head whipped to the side, his attention focused, his nostrils flared. "The man who follows you...what did you see?"

Sarah stared into the darkness, unable to find the target of his attention. The street was empty save for the two of them, houses rising on either side. "Sometimes I saw a man-shaped shadow. Sometimes I heard footsteps. Tonight, I saw him, a shape, a form, indistinct. He wore a hat that hid his face..." She shook her head, then spun to her right, an eerie sensation crawling across her skin.

Killian was there, on her right, though an instant ago he had been on her left. She hadn't seen him move.

"He does not approach you?" There was tension in his tone.

"He shrinks back when I face him, as though he is wary of confronting me directly."

Killian's lips drew back, baring his teeth and he prowled around her, blocking her view of the street, using his body as a shield. He made a sound such as she had never before heard—a snarl, a growl, a bestial warning. It made the hackles rise on the back of her neck. He seemed to grow in size, his shoulders broader, his chest wider. Here were threat and power. Here was the man she had sensed lurking beneath the façade. But none of the threat was aimed at her. It was aimed at the street and whatever danger lurked in the darkness.

"Do you see him?" she asked, her voice low.

"Inside, if you please, Sarah," he said. "Now."

Deciding that she was destined to lose any further argument, she turned and led the way to the front door. It seemed that Killian Thayne would be accompanying her to her room. Modesty, propriety, her good name...she might have presented any of those as reasons he must not come inside. But, in truth, what was the point? The other lodgers in the house on Coptic Street would have no care if she brought a man to her room. She knew for certain that one of the girls did exactly that on a regular basis and slipped Mrs. Cowden an extra shilling each week so that she would turn a blind eye.

Pausing at the door, she looked back at him over her shoulder. *Killian*. He bid her call him Killian, as she had a thousand times in her dreams.

"You are safe with me, Sarah."

No, she did not think so.

But she knew he meant to reassure her that he was not the one who had chased her through the alleys, and *that* was the truth.

"You have no hat."

His eyes narrowed at her observation. "Does the lack offend?"

Sarah made a soft, chuffing laugh. "Taking offense at some nicety of fashion is a luxury for which I have no use." She pressed her lips together. "It was only an observation."

"Because your pursuer wore a hat."

"Yes. You seek to reassure me, but such reassurance is unnecessary. We already established that you were not my pursuer."

Killian caught her wrist as she reached for the doorknob. "I am not he. Had I chosen to hunt you, Sarah, you would not have known I was there." He paused, his lips curving into a dark smile. "And I would have caught you."

Had I chosen to hunt you. A chill crawled up her spine, one that had nothing to do with the wind or the cold. She looked beyond him to the street once more, then away.

"Is it your intent to make me fear you?"

"Fear me?" He looked appalled. "Quite the opposite, though I have clearly made a hash of it." His laugh was low and devoid of humor. "Once, I had skill at this. I knew the rules of the game." The way he looked at her made her breath catch.

She was left with no doubt that the game he referred to was flirtation. A thrill ran through her, equal parts attraction and wariness.

Seeking to alleviate the tension of the moment, she said, "I shall be lucky if Mrs. Cowden kept a plate for me this evening, but if she did, I will be glad to share my meal with you."

An indecipherable emotion danced across Killian's features. "Your offer is most kind, but I have...already dined."

The slight hesitation did not go unnoticed, and she wondered what his words masked. He offered nothing further and after a moment, she turned back to unlock the door.

She led him inside. The hallway was dark, musty, the paint yellowed and flaking, the floor a tiled geometric pattern of gray and black. Sarah thought that once, many years ago, the pattern might have been white and black, but layers of wear and use and grime had altered the shade. Mrs. Cowden occasionally swiped a mop over the tile with halfhearted interest, but that only served to shift the dirt from left to right and back again. The hallway was so cramped that they could not stand side by side, and Sarah went in first with Killian close behind.

She felt glad that she was not alone.

No, more than that, glad that *he* was here. It was a dangerous and inappropriate gladness that bubbled inside her like the effervescent spring water her father had insisted was good for the health.

Turning back, she was confronted by Killian's cloak-draped form, so broad and tall. He unnerved her. Drew her. Appealed to her on some level she could not explain. His presence made her feel safe. How long since she had felt that way?

Hoping that her expression betrayed none of her inappropriate thoughts, she reached around him to draw the door closed, an action that brought them far closer together than they ought to be. He was warm, the heat coming from him beckoning to her.

"How are you so warm?" she asked. "It's bitingly cold outside, and you've been in the wind just the same as I."

"My meal warmed me," he said after a pause.

An odd reply.

Stepping back, she undid the fastening of her cloak but did not draw the garment off. Though the wind was absent, the hallway was barely warmer than it was outdoors, and she was loath to forfeit whatever heat her cloak offered.

Directly ahead lay the rickety staircase with the faulty third stair, the one with the poorly nailed board that would pop up and bang the unwary person sharply on the ankle if they were not careful. There was room enough for one person to go up or down, but not enough for two to pass unless they turned to face each other.

There was no light coming from the dining room, and none showed under the crack of the door that led to Mrs. Cowden's chambers. Sarah was glad of that, for it meant there was none about to beg explanation for Killian's inexplicable presence here.

"I will be but a moment," Sarah said and strode beyond the stairs to the small kitchen at the back of the house. No candles were lit, but the hearth held a faltering flame, and Sarah moved close to warm her hands. Closing her eyes, she let the heat sink through her.

He made no sound, but she knew he had followed. Stepping to the side, she glanced at him over her shoulder. The glow of the dying embers danced over his features, painting him gold and bronze and more beautiful than any man had a right to be.

"Here," she said, beckoning him closer. "There's room enough for both of us. The night is so cold. You must be frozen clear through."

"No." He made a small smile, looking more handsome still because of it. "I am not cold. I do not notice such things. Neither the cold of winter nor the heat of summer."

"You are an adaptable fellow."

"That is one way to describe it." He glanced about the tiny kitchen, his gaze lingering on the covered plate set on one side of the small table. "You must be hungry."

She shook her head. She wasn't. The fright of earlier in the evening had left her insides shaking still. "I'll take the plate up with me and eat a bit later."

"Where are your rooms?" he asked.

"Rooms?" she echoed. "Only one, I'm afraid. But it suits well enough. I'm on the second floor."

She took the plate and led the way from the warm kitchen back into the cold hallway, up the stairs to the landing on the first floor, then up another flight to the second.

"How many rooms up here?" Killian asked, his voice hushed, the sound incredibly appealing.

"Three. And three on the floor below." She unlocked the door of her chamber and pushed it open. "I have the smallest of these. It was the frugal choice." Why had she said that?

"Ever practical," he said, sounding as though the words pained him. But his expression gave her no insight into his thoughts.

"Spinster sisters share the room next to mine. They snore."

"Yes. I hear that," he said with another small smile.

Sarah smiled back, the tension knotting her shoulders unlocking. "It usually reaches a crescendo just past midnight and then they quiet down." Setting the plate on the little tulip table in the corner near the door, she then took up a Lucifer match, struck it to the sandpaper and lit the stub of tallow candle that sat in a small porcelain dish with gold edging, one of the few possessions she had salvaged from the shattered remnants of her old life.

The flame flickered and wavered, barely denting the darkness. She turned to face Killian, who filled the doorway like a shadow.

What to do now? Invite him inside? There seemed no help for it, but she felt so odd to be in this situation, to have him here in this dim and crowded room. He had been here before, but only in her mind, her dreams, her fantasies.

The reality of him was overwhelming, as were the events of the evening, being chased, fleeing, arriving home to find him here.

"Come in," she said, suddenly weary.

He did as she bid, stepping inside and pulling the door shut behind him.

🦋 12 🦋

He controlled himself with effort. The monster inside him quivered and roared, anxious to be out, to hunt. Not to feed, but to find and destroy the one who stalked her, frightened her.

Sarah.

She was not mistaken in her assessment that she was hunted.

She only did not realize precisely what it was that hunted her. But he knew. He sensed it out there, like to like.

He wanted to kill it, to rip open its throat.

Not only because such was the instinct of his kind, though there was that.

No, he wanted it gone because it posed a threat to her. *No one harms her. No one.*

She is mine.

13

Killian filled the space, sucked the air from the room even as he ener-
gized it. His eyes locked on Sarah's, glittering in the candlelight, and
her heart beat so hard she thought it might fly apart. She dropped her
gaze and toyed with the remnants of the match; she could not look at
him, did not dare to look at him, for so many twined and tangled
reasons.

"You are cold," Killian observed, stepping closer, and before she
could protest he had his cloak off his own shoulders and over hers, still
warm from the heat of his body, smelling faintly of citrus and man.

His action highlighted one of the many reasons she admired him
so. Because he would do something like that for her. Because he
offered similar quiet kindnesses to many. She had seen it time and
again on the ward with patients, and even with staff. Though his tone
was usually cool and analytical, his treatment choices unaffected by
emotion, his overtures at camaraderie with his contemporaries limited
at best, there were small things he did that showed the warmth
beneath his icy façade.

There had been the episode with Mrs. Carmichael when he had
gifted her with the coats for her sons. And she had seen him slip coins
in another night nurse's apron while she slept, a shilling or two, enough

to buy shrimps and tea and butter. He had sat the night through beside a mother whose daughter would never awaken, holding her hand as her child slipped away. And Sarah suspected it was Killian who had arranged for Mr. Scully's sister to travel to Edinburgh to stay with his dead wide's sister so neither would be alone.

Killian was an outwardly cold man with a flame inside him that he hid behind darkened spectacles and a mask of polite reserve.

She wondered if he was lonely or simply alone.

She stared up at him, feeling foolish and overwhelmed and so grateful for this small kindness. Tears pricked her eyes as she huddled in his cloak and that made her angry. She had no place in her life for self-pity, and after crying for three days straight when she found out her father was dead, she had thought herself moved past such a childish waste of time.

"Tell me why you came here tonight," she said, pushing aside her maudlin thoughts and pitching her voice low so as not to carry through the thin walls.

"Let us sit, Sarah." Reasonable. Calm.

His words made her anxious. Sit where? On the low bed? Uneasy, she cast a glance exactly there, and for a moment, she could not understand what it was she saw on her pillow.

Then she *did* understand and fear curdled in her belly.

On her pillow was a small comfit box of sweetmeats tied with a bow and beside it, a length of lavender ribbon.

She gasped and stumbled back, the very familiarity of those things making them all the more sinister.

Someone had been here. In her room. Someone had left these unwelcome gifts. Someone who knew things about her. An icy chill slithered through her, distress clenching around her heart.

"What is it?" Killian asked sharply, drawing near. "You've gone white as the belly of a dead fish."

Sarah's gaze jerked to his, and despite the unease that gnawed at her she could not help the startled chuff of laughter evoked by his words.

"An appealing image." Dead fish. She shuddered, thinking of her father, his body never fished from the Thames. Never found.

The shudders would not stop, though she willed them to.

Killian closed his hands around her upper arms and kept them there as she trembled. She wished he would draw her closer, not just clasp her arms, but clasp her body tight against his own.

She pulled away from him, wrapping her arms around her middle and holding tight. "You left me the pasty. That day in the linen closet."

"I did." He frowned. "You had not eaten."

"And the orange? The ham sandwich? You left me those as well?"

Still, he frowned. "The sandwich, yes." The word was slow and drawn out, as though he took his time trying to read the underlying thoughts beneath her words. "The orange, no."

"Then who?" she asked.

"That is the question, is it not?"

"And those?" She flung a hand toward the bed. "Did you bring those? Why not just hand them to me? Why leave them on my pillow?" Her words came faster now, strung together in a furious whisper. "And why slink into my chamber and leave them on my bed then sneak back outside to await my arrival?"

"Sneak..." he looked to the bed, then back to her. "Sarah, this is the first time I have been in this room." He crossed to the bed and lifted the small box and the length of ribbon. She flinched away. He opened the confit box to reveal caramels and marchpane.

Someone had chosen the contents with care. Someone who knew her ways and her preferences.

"You didn't bring them?" she asked, her voice tight.

"I did not. But someone did..." He looked at her expectantly as though she ought to know the identity of that someone.

And she did. "It was him." The man who stalked her, who clung to the shadows, who refused to reveal his face. He had chased her through the alleys tonight, but first he had come here. "He was in my room," she whispered. "He touched my things. He must have left me the orange as well. He's been watching me here, at the hospital...everywhere."

Killian's expression darkened. He held the confit box in one hand, the ribbon in the other.

"Sweetmeats. Ribbon. Impersonal at first glance, but first glance is a lie," he said. "These items have specific meaning to you."

"Yes." Sarah felt ill, confused...afraid. "Someone knows far too much about me. Someone knows things that are private, things from my life before my father died. My father used to bring me ribbons and that very same selection of sweetmeats before he became...ill."

Killian's gaze flicked to the items he held, then back to her face. "The man who stalks you, how long has he been about it?"

Sarah frowned, thinking back. "The first time I saw him was a few weeks after my father died."

Killian set the box and ribbon on the bed. "That was the first time you *saw* him. But before that..."

"I sensed him. I knew he was there. I thought it was grief that played tricks on my perception. I *felt* someone watching me, following me, always in the shadows."

"The first time...When was it?"

Again, she thought back, trying to piece together the puzzle. "I don't know. I think the first sense I had of someone lurking was..." She had cried for three days and not left the house. But on the fourth day she had forced herself out in the evening, forced herself to walk along the river, and she had looked over her shoulder more than once, plagued by an eerie feeling that she was being followed. "You think he has been following me all along? Even before I sensed his presence?"

"You said your father was ill. What malady afflicted him?" Killian asked.

There was something in his tone, an urgency she couldn't understand. Her chin kicked up a notch. "He became addicted to opium."

Everything about Killian stilled: his movements, his expression. He looked to be made of stone. "How do you know it was opium?"

"He took no food. He said everything made him sick to his stomach. Everything tasted rotten and foul. His complexion took on a terrible grayish cast. He spiraled into malaise."

"How long was he like that?"

"I don't know. It felt like an instant even as it felt like forever. Months and months. By the end, he clung to the shadows and eschewed the light. Sunlight made him cry out in pain. Lamplight made him wince."

"What else?" Killian asked, his attention focused and intense. Frightening.

"He was too ill himself to see patients. He spent his days abed in a darkened room, and his nights prowling the streets, or perhaps in opium dens."

"Did he hurt you?" Killian asked.

"No... No!" Sarah shivered. "But one night, I thought he might," she admitted after a long pause, relieved to finally tell someone. "He was ill in his bed, muttering and cursing and pleading, though I know not for what. He was drenched in sweat. I went to change his night-shirt and as I leaned over him, he caught my wrist, his grip far stronger than I would have expected from one so ill. He stared at me. I was—" She broke off, remembering. Her father had looked at her through eyes that were not his own.

"You were..." Killian prodded.

"Afraid," Sarah whispered, hating the admission, hating that the harsh memory was one of her last of her father. "I was afraid of him. My gentle, kind father was not there. Someone else looked back at me through his eyes." She exhaled in a huff. "You think me melodramatic."

Killian stepped closer. "I think you brave. Resourceful. A woman carving her way in an unkind world."

The way he looked at her made her pulse race and her mouth go dry. She made a nervous laugh and looked at the ground. "My father... the look on his face was one I had never seen. He looked like he would do me harm, like he *wanted* to do me harm. He cried out as though in pain and thrust me from him. He snarled at me and said that I was never to come into his chamber again. Not while he was in it. 'Get out. Get out now,' he shouted though he was never one to raise his voice. I ran and moments later watched from my window as he went out into the night with his nightshirt flapping and his feet bare."

Killian took another step toward her, but Sarah shook her head and stumbled back. If he touched her now, she would break, shatter, and she would never be able to knit the jagged pieces back together.

"How did he take his opium? Laudanum? Some other tincture? A pipe?" he asked.

"I don't know. He took it privately. I never saw."

"And after he died? You found no bottles? No pipe?"

Sarah closed her eyes for an instant, picturing their house, her father's chamber. "No. I found nothing. He must have taken the drug elsewhere. At an opium den."

"Or not at all," Killian said.

"What do you mean? You think my assessment incorrect? You have some other explanation for his symptoms? There is no other disease I know of that would explain it. If you know such a one, educate me. I beg you." As the last word left her lips, Sarah realized she spoke too fast, too loud. She wanted Killian to tell her of such a disease, to absolve her father of the addiction Sarah had attributed to him.

But Killian offered no such kindness. Instead, he asked, "The night he went out in his bare feet... Was that the last time you saw him?"

"No. I saw him early the next morning, before dawn. I was restless, unable to sleep. I went to the kitchen to make tea. He sat there in the dark. When I came in, he looked up at me and smiled. He was himself in that moment. He was the father I had always known.

"He seemed a different man than he had been the night before. Physically, at least. His skin was ruddy, his movements sure. But he was tormented, apologizing again and again for his actions, for frightening me. I said I forgave him. I made to touch his hand, but he backed away. He told me I must never again come into his chamber when he was there. He was adamant, distressed. He said I must stay away when he descended into what he called his melancholy." She swallowed, the memories making her chest ache and her throat thick. It was both a torture and a relief to talk with someone about her father's death. Before this, there had been no one to tell. "Two nights later, he drowned. His body was not recovered."

"How came you to know of his death?" Killian asked, his voice gentle.

"Several witnesses saw him tumble into the Thames, including my father's old friend, Dr. Grammercy, a man I know and trust. Though I had no body to bury and mourn, I had their testimony, the gruesome truth of it." Sarah paused, replaying the entirety of their conversation in her thoughts. "Do you think the man who hunts me was a patient of my father's?"

"Perhaps."

"Someone from the opium den?"

"Perhaps."

She did not take his replies as evasive. He only spoke the truth. It could be a man from either of those sources or neither.

Killian glanced over his shoulder. "You locked your door when you left this morning?"

"Yes. And you watched me unlock it just now."

His attention flicked to the window. "He came in by other means." He reached for the spare blanket she kept folded at the foot of her bed, shook it out, and wrapped it around her shoulders. She realized then that she was shaking, her teeth chattering.

Killian stood mere inches away. She had to battle the urge to lean in against him, to rest her cheek against his chest and let the sound of his heartbeat ease her worries. Instead, she forced herself to step away from him. He did not follow, but she thought he wanted to. She thought he wanted to hold her as desperately as she wanted to be held.

The backs of her legs brushed the spindly chair in the corner. She sank down and stared up at him, her thoughts a muddle of wary confusion.

There was no sense in any of this. Not in the pursuer who dogged her every step. Not in the gifts left on her pillow. And not in the attention shown her by Killian Thayne.

She yet had no idea why he was here. She wasn't certain she wanted to know. He came to her home, alone, at night...

"I think you should go," she said, and rose to drag off first the blanket, then his cloak, the latter of which she held out to him. His brows drew together as he took the cloak from her and draped it over his forearm. Then he lifted the discarded blanket and wrapped it around her shoulders once more.

"I cannot go." His hard mouth curved up a little. "I am afraid that my damnably chivalrous nature precludes my leaving you here alone tonight."

For an instant, she made no reply, her thoughts spinning through a thousand remembered dreams where he had been in this room with her, his lips on hers. She took a slow breath and forced herself to speak. "What are you suggesting?"

"I suggest nothing. I state fact. I will remain here with you—"

"—you cannot—" She shook her head.

"—or you will accompany me to my home—"

"—I cannot—"

"—and I beg you to cease interrupting my every word."

"My apologies," she offered acerbically, not bothering to mask the fact that her words were insincere. "You cannot simply step into my life and tell me what I will and will not do. I do not answer to you, sir."

"No, you do not," he murmured and shot her an indecipherable look. "I wonder if you have ever answered to anyone." There was a measure of admiration in his tone.

"There was a time that I relied on my father's decisions and good counsel to guide my life. Then he began to make only bad decisions, and finally, none at all, and so I learned to make my own." She crossed to the bed where she scooped up both the ribbon and the box. She strode to the door, opened it, and set both out on the floor outside the door of the snoring sisters, then stepped back inside and closed her own door behind her.

Turning to face him once more, she rested her back against the wood and made a noisy, rushed exhalation.

"Well," he said, his tone laced with humor. "That was a solution."

"The best I could conjure at the moment."

"You are ever resourceful." Again, the whisper of admiration. It made her feel as though he *knew* her, saw the practical, intelligent part of her and valued that.

The moment spun out, thin and fragile, her thoughts battling within her. The imaginary Killian of her dreams would step closer, embrace her, press his lips to her temple. But this was no imaginary lover, and she thought that if the real Killian Thayne drew her into his embrace, he would do far more than kiss her temple.

She sighed in both relief and disappointment when he moved to the far wall with its two tall, narrow windows. He shifted the curtain to the side, staring out into the night. A low sound came from him, almost a growl. A warning.

"What do you see?" she asked.

"Nothing." But he did not move from the window. Finally, he checked the latch and, satisfied, drew the frayed and moth-eaten velvet curtain shut. With a step to the right, he faced the second window and tested the latch. It slid free and the pane swung open, letting in a swirling blast of frigid air.

He did not so much as blink as the wind hit him. With careful attention, he closed the window and tested the latch, then played with it a moment until it clicked into place. It was merely temperamental, but not broken. He did not draw the curtain. Instead, he stood close to the glass, looking out, and Sarah had the same impression she had had outdoors—that he somehow appeared even taller, broader...a threat, but not to her.

"Is he out there?" she asked.

His gaze sought hers. "I am staying."

The temptation to sink into the safety of his presence and simply thank him and let him do as he wished was a succulent lure. But she refused to be beguiled. To accept his comfort tonight meant that tomorrow night it would be all the more difficult to discover comfort on her own.

"While I appreciate your kind offer, there is no need for you to remain here. I have spent many nights alone in this place, and I awaken each morning with my heart yet beating and breath in my lungs. This night will be no different. I think it best if you go."

Eyes the color of a storm-laden sky pinned her and held her in place. "I will sit on that chair, or I will take you to my home and you may spend the night there. The choice is yours."

"You cannot spend the night in this room. My room."

"As you wish," he agreed amiably and grabbed the chair from the corner. He carried it to the door. "I shall spend the night on the landing outside your door."

"There is no need," she insisted once more. "I shall be perfectly safe here with the windows latched and the door locked."

"I beg to differ. There are creatures of the night that even the best locks will not hold at bay."

The way he said that, soft and menacing, set a shiver crawling up her spine.

"You cannot sleep in the hard chair." She stepped forward and laid her hand next to his on the chair back.

"I need little sleep." The smile he turned on her was languid, and it made her pulse trip. "I will stay the night through and leave at the first hint of dawn before the house awakens. No one will know I was here, and you will be safe in the light."

She held her place, held his gaze, her heart racing a wild, heady pace. "Safe in the light? I don't understand."

"I know. And I am not yet ready to explain." His smile dropped away, and he took a slow deep breath, his chest expanding, his gaze gliding over her in a lazy caress, lingering on her lips in a way that made her pulse pound hard and fast. "I hear your blood rushing in your veins, Sarah."

How could he possibly hear that? And yet, it sounded as though he spoke the truth. She made a stunted, nervous laugh.

His hand shifted on the chair until it covered her own. Warm skin. She could not think, could not breathe.

"Is it for me that your heart races?" he whispered, his voice warm and rough.

For him. Yes.

He leaned in, his cheek almost touching hers.

"Sarah." Her name was a breath. A whisper. A question.

She held her silence, uncertain what answer to give.

"I have enjoyed every conversation, every interaction. I enjoy the way your mouth twists a little to the right when you are deep in thought." He touched his fingertip to the corner of her mouth. She gasped and had the strangest urge to open her lips and lick his skin. "I enjoy the way you walk with purpose, head high. I enjoy the sound of your laughter when you tease Mrs. Bayley, and the tone of your voice when you offer kindness to a dying man." He brushed her cheek with the backs of his knuckles and she leaned into his touch. "I had not planned it, this fascination. But here it is—" his chin brushed against her hair as he leaned closer, and her heart stopped, her breath stopped "—and I find myself glad of it, though reason argues it is unwise."

Her senses hummed with her awareness of him, with the warm glow that swelled at his words and the wild ache that spread through her limbs.

Oh, her mind was not her own, her body heavy and hot.

She wanted him to kiss her. Wanted to know the feel and taste of him. She was hungry for him, her lips tingling, her belly lit from inside with a heat that bordered on pain. Even in her inexperience, she recognized the feeling for what it was. Attraction. Desire.

It was lovely, this feeling, lovely and frightening and thrilling. She thought that if only he would press his mouth to hers that she would understand, would know secrets that hovered just beyond her reach.

He turned to her then, his movement quick, and she fell back a step, her back pressed to the wall.

Both hands shot out and Killian laid his palms flat against the wall on either side of her shoulders. She held herself still, her heart thundering, her gaze locked on his mouth, and he smiled, a dark, dangerous curving of his lips that bared a flash of white teeth for but an instant.

"You crave my touch." Not a question. She was glad. She had no breath left to form an answer.

Taking his weight on his outstretched arms and flattened palms, he leaned in and brushed her lips with his, soft, gentle. Their bodies touched nowhere but their lips and she was undone by that caress.

Fire roared through her veins. She was so focused on him that the world beyond faded away to nothing.

His tongue traced the seam of her mouth, and when she gasped in shock, he pushed inside, his tongue *inside* her, tasting her, touching her.

She moaned, stunned by the wild kaleidoscope of sensation, endlessly wondrous.

Winding her arms around his neck she tunneled her fingers in his hair, enjoying the sensation of the silky strands running through her fingers. She kissed him back, following his lead. Tentatively, she touched her tongue to his, then grew bolder, stroking him and learning the feel of his mouth.

His weight came down on her, the lush heat of his body, making her blood rush and her belly dance with a low, humming ache. He curved his arms around her, one hand flat against the small of her back, the other cupping her bottom. She raised up on her toes, driven by instinct to mold herself to him, to fit every ridge and edge of him in the soft swells and dips of her body, his thighs hard against her own, his belly and chest taut where hers were soft. She found exquisite pleasure in the weight of him pressing her to the wall at her back.

He kissed her jaw, her neck, his mouth lingering on the pulse that beat there, his breathing ragged. Arching back, she offered herself, loving the sensation of his lips at her throat, his teeth grazing the tender skin.

With a groan, he tensed then drew back, his eyes gone dark, the pupils dilated.

Panting, she stared up at him, understanding neither herself in that moment nor the wild, turbulent, emotions rolling about inside her like heavy charcoal-limned clouds in a storm.

He meant to turn away. She sensed that. Meant to block out the wonderful connection that spun out between them, a glittering thread.

"I feel as though I stand on the edge of a cliff, the wind whipping my cloak behind me, and if I can only find the will and courage to leap, I will fly," she whispered. "Kiss me again, Killian. Make me fly."

She was drunk on the taste of him, the feel of him, unlike anything she had ever experienced.

The look he turned on her was feral. Hungry. She thought he would plunder her, take her, drag her against him and kiss her in ways she was too untutored to imagine.

Yearning sluiced through her, fever bright.

And she thought her heart would break when he stepped away, mastering himself with visible effort, his cool mask sliding in place to obscure the burning heat she knew she had not mistaken.

"Sarah," he rasped, his gaze locked on her throat, hot and dark. Slowly, he raised his eyes to hers. "I must not—"

He shook his head, and she felt lost, barren, already missing the connection that melted away. He brushed his thumb along her cheek and she ached to fling herself against him.

Rooted in place, she watched as he took a step toward the door, then paused to look back at her over his shoulder, his eyes gone flat and dark, fathomless, mysterious, too many secrets reflected back at her. She was so attuned to him in this impossible moment, she *felt* the leashed tension inside him.

There had been a thrilling edge of desperation in that kiss. Need. Hunger. She ached to untether the bonds he set about himself, to follow where that desperation might lead.

A perilous path to tread; a most dangerous thing to want.

14

Killian held her gaze a moment longer, his hands held in tight fists at his sides, his control clearly in place, if somewhat tattered. Sarah recognized that she affected him and that pleased her. The realization was disconcerting.

"Lock the door behind me," he said, his voice taut.

She had no wish to lock the door against him. She had no wish for him to leave at all. Her lips felt warm, swollen from his kiss, and she wanted only to press her mouth to his and kiss him again.

"If I lock the door, how will you come to me should I call out?" Such a reasonable question, despite the unreasonable circumstance. She could not imagine calling out to him, could not imagine him sitting out there all night on the small, stiff chair. Why would he do that for her?

His shoulders tensed, but he did not look at her again. "There is no door that could stop me if I wanted to be at your side, Sarah. Remember that. Remember that I—" he made a slow exhalation, as though he struggled with the words, and after an instant, he continued in a low, ragged tone "—I am not like other men."

No, he was not. A part of her recognized that with soul-searing clarity. He was like no one she had ever known. She had long sensed a hidden part of him, held in careful check just beneath the surface, and she did not doubt that he spoke the truth, that no lock, no door could hold him. It was a strange and frightening comfort.

He walked past the small table with the candle and the plate of food, and he paused there, his attention snared. She thought he meant to insist she eat, and she knew that she could not. Her stomach was alternately in knots, or dancing and twisting like it held a thousand butterflies struggling to get free.

"What is this?" he asked, lifting the old and yellowed copy of *New Monthly* magazine that lay open beside the plate. He read aloud the title of the short story she had pored over so many times that she could recite it by heart. "*The Vampyre* by John William Polidori—" he glanced at the date "—April 1, 1819."

His voice had grown eerily flat, devoid of inflection.

"My father was obsessed with that story before his death," Sarah said. "He read it again and again, studying and dissecting the words as though they held the secret mysteries of life." She shook her head. "I have read it myself so many times that I can recite it in its entirety. A sad and horrid tale, but I do not see what agitated my father so greatly. There are no secrets hidden there."

"Are there not?" He cast her a veiled look. "May I take this to read while I keep watch?"

Keep watch. Over her. When was the last time she had felt safe? Months. Perhaps years. But tonight, with Killian guarding her door, she was safe.

She knew not how to place that fact in the twisted uncertainty that had become her life.

"Yes, please do. Perhaps in your reading, you will find the secrets that I missed."

"Perhaps. Tell me, in the end, is the vampire revealed for the monster he is?"

"Yes. How did you know?"

"A guess. Are vampires not always fiends?" The thread of irony in his tone gave her pause.

"I don't know. I have not read many such tales."

He nodded slowly. "You have not read Byron's *The Giaour*?"

"I have not."

"It is a poem about a monster damned to drain life from those it loves." There was no inflection to his words. They were flat and dry, yet she thought they meant something to him.

"How terrible," she said. "To be so damned and so alone in that damnation."

His gaze burned into her. "You feel pity for the monster?"

She swallowed. Did she? "Yes." She looked at the floor. "Such loneliness is a vile pestilence eating one from the inside out." She looked up again. "Perhaps he was a monster because of his loneliness."

Killian drummed his fingers in a slow roll across the tabletop, and she had the feeling that he argued a silent debate within himself, as though he meant to say something and weighed the pros and cons. In the end, he said, "I...*dislike* that you know anything about such loneliness."

Her gaze shot to his. "And I dislike that you know it too," she whispered, daring much with this assumption.

He did not argue her assertion; he inclined his head and exited her chamber, closing the door behind him with a soft snick.

She hesitated then went to the door, pressing her palms against the frame. She could not say how she knew it, but she did—she knew he waited, listening until she turned the key in the lock.

Her hand trembled, and she held it out flat, watching the fluttering movement, feeling the reflection of that quaking in her soul. With a sigh, she rested her forehead against the wood and imagined that on the far side of the door, Killian leaned in and did the same.

A moment later, she heard the creak of the chair as he sat, and it was only then that she recalled there was no light on the landing, and Killian had taken no candle.

She wondered how he would read the story of *The Vampyre* in the dark.

MUTED SOUNDS CARRIED FROM BELOW WHEN SARAH AWAKENED THE following morning. The house was stirring. Shards of light stole through the crack where the ancient, frayed curtains met. Recalling all that had passed the previous night, the fear of being hunted, the thrill of being kissed, she gathered her resolve and crossed to the door. Throwing it open, she found Killian gone from the hallway, and *The Vampyre* resting on the chair.

He must have left at the first sign of dawn as he had promised. She was both disappointed and relieved by that. Relieved, too, because the confit box and ribbon were gone. Either the sisters had discovered the items or Killian had taken them away, a small but welcome kindness.

She washed and dressed with haste, for the hour was later than she preferred. Soon, she walked briskly along Portugal Street toward the hospital, her thoughts consumed by recollections of all that had passed between her and Killian, her emotions in a terrible state of confusion. Questions scurried about in her mind like the mice in the hallways of King's College. She had run the gamut last night from abject terror as the unknown man chased her through the alleys, to absolute bliss as Killian kissed her, his mouth hot and hungry on her own.

His kiss had aroused both her body and her mind, weaving her in a spell of delicious wonder. His abrupt withdrawal had left her adrift, uncertain what to think, what to feel.

One thing she did know was that, oddly, last night she had slept better than any night since her father's drowning, and she was grateful to Killian for that. After the terror she had endured during her panic-scored flight to Coptic Street, it was only the knowledge that he guarded her that had allowed her to sink into sweet slumber, and once there, she had dreamed of him.

There was danger in allowing herself to succumb to the lure of his protection, for who would watch over her tonight and in the nights to come? Only herself, as it had been only herself for so many months now. She was proud of that, of her ability to find solutions and care for herself in a city that was far from kind to a woman alone. Still, the luxury of allowing herself to be protected for a single night had been a sweet and wonderful balm.

And a distraction.

In the end, she had never learned why Killian had waited for her outside Mrs. Cowden's house, the question of that forgotten in the muddle of other concerns and the heady lure of his kiss.

She was left wondering about that this morning as she made her way along the street, about his reasons for seeking her out last night.

Better to think of that than to ponder their late-night confessions where each had owned the paucity of their lives, the emptiness, the loneliness. She knew why she was alone. In part, it was the life she had led with her father, one which had offered few opportunities to cultivate friendships. In part, it was the lack of relatives. And in part, it was by choice for while she did not doubt she could find a man to marry her, she had no wish to marry a man who would limit her life to the four walls of their home, to washing his laundry and cooking his meals. No, she was better off alone and working at King's College, which at least offered her opportunities to learn, to expand her knowledge, to care for others who needed her.

But better off or not, she was not merely alone. She was lonely, aching for someone to talk to, to laugh with, to cry with, to love.

Still, it was better to live a life of poverty and loneliness than to sacrifice the person she was.

Reaching the hospital, she hurried inside, out of the biting wind. After hanging her cloak away, she went to the sick ward and found Elinor there ahead of her, setting out bowls on the tray.

The other woman set aside her task and hurried over to grab Sarah's arm and draw her to one side. "Have you heard?" the widow asked in a low voice, her eyes wide and round. Her words suggested she had a new tidbit of gossip to share, but her expression and tone belied that. Elinor was disturbed, afraid, and the words she shared were a cry of distress. "There's been another death. This one worse than the others. The victim's throat was torn open, and still not a drop of blood to be found." She tightened her grip on Sarah's arm. "Explain that by bugs and fever and excoriation, if you can, Sarah Lowell."

Reeling with the horror of Elinor's words, Sarah stood frozen in mute dismay. A greasy knot of dread congealed in her gut. Finally, she managed to croak, "Where?"

"Surgical ward. Mr. Simon found him an hour ago."

An hour ago. Before dawn. "What was Mr. Simon doing here so early? He usually comes in past nine."

"He said he had concern for the patient he trephined yesterday. Wanted to see how he had weathered the night."

Sarah held very still, sensing the answer before she even asked the question. "And how had he weathered the night?"

"He's the one who is dead." Her reply scratched at Sarah's composure and sent a whisper of icy foreboding curling through her veins. Elinor darted a quick look around the ward and dropped her voice even further. "Yesterday, Mr. Simon and Mr. Thayne had words over that patient. Mr. Thayne said that the man had been insensate for over a week since he fell from the roof of the Bull and Mouth Inn, that he was unresponsive to stimulus of any kind, even pain. Mr. Thayne said he wasn't likely to get any better if Mr. Simon drilled a hole in his skull. But Mr. Simon said there was no way to know for certain and so he went ahead and did it anyway."

"And today the man is dead."

"Not just dead." Elinor pressed her lips into a tight line. "Murdered. There can be no doubt of it now, no simple explanations, or even convoluted ones, to brush aside concerns."

Sarah stared at her, then looked around the ward. The patients were restless and wary, watching them, straining to hear their words. "Everyone knows?" she asked.

Elinor nodded.

"I must see—"

Elinor nodded again. "Go on."

Without another word, Sarah spun and strode down the hall to the surgical ward, skidding to a halt just inside the doors. She stood, trembling, her heart hammering, her palms damp.

A group of men huddled around a bed in the middle of the large room, among them Mr. Simon and Mr. Franks, and two men she thought must be constables from the Metropolitan Police. One of them—dark haired and swarthy—seemed familiar, and she wondered if he was the officer who had attended the ward before, the one who had declined Elinor's offer of tea.

"I tell you, sir, that I saw Mr. Thayne lurking about when I left last night," said Mr. Simon.

"And what time was that?" asked the constable.

"Just before midnight. I know it because as I walked through the front doors, I heard the clock strike the hour."

"And did you speak with Mr. Thayne at that time?"

"I did not. But I believe it was he that I saw."

"You *believe* it was he?" the second constable asked. "Did you see him or not?"

Mr. Simon's lips thinned, and when he spoke his voice was high with irritation, his cheeks flushed red. "I did not see his face clearly, but I saw enough of him to determine his identity. The man was tall, as is Mr. Thayne."

"As am I. As is that attendant there." The dark-haired constable gestured at a man standing by the wall and then cocked his head to one side. "You and Mr. Thayne are of a similar height, are you not?"

"Similar height. Different build. I tell you the culprit is Mr. Thayne," Mr. Simon insisted. "He has been on this ward each time someone died of the strange and inexplicable wounds perpetrated upon their bodies. He and I had words over the care of each of those patients. And—"

"—and I would like to know precisely what accusations are leveled against me," Killian said in a ringing voice as he stepped through the second doorway on the far side of the ward. His gaze slid to Sarah, lingered for an instant before sliding away. He scanned the faces of the men assembled around the corpse.

Sarah watched him walk deeper into the room, thinking that he seemed to appear mid-conversation with odd regularity, as though he could hear others invoking his name from a great distance. The thought flickered and then slipped away as Mr. Simon said, "Mr. Thayne, you will confirm your whereabouts last night." The constable cast him a sidelong glance. Mr. Simon's chest puffed up. "He was here each time a patient was killed," he said to the constable, then looked to Mr. Franks for confirmation.

Mr. Franks, ever true to his adversarial nature, stepped forward and said, "As was I. As were you. As were the night nurses and several of the apprentices." His attention was snared by a man on the far side of the bed. "Like young Mr. Watts there, with his white bib apron. I am certain you were here last night, were you not? You went out and then returned. I saw you come back with a sour face, saw you doff your gloves and hat and hang your cloak."

Mr. Watts looked at the ground. Sarah studied him for a moment. He was tall and broad in the shoulders. And he was the apprentice Elinor had mentioned, the one she claimed watched Sarah with interest of a romantic nature. It was true, Sarah realized in that moment. Mr. Watts *did* watch her and he was always at the hospital when she was. He raised his head now and met her gaze. There was something dark there, something...angry.

According to Mr. Franks, Mr. Watts had left King's College last night only to return.

Could he be the man who followed her?

Could he be the killer?

"Valid points," Killian said as he stepped deeper into the room, holding to the shadows, out of the spill of morning light that came through the window. "I was here, as was Mr. Franks and Mr. Watts and a dozen others. As were you, Mr. Simon. Does that bring you under equal suspicion?"

"It does not." Mr. Simon's words fell like drops of burning acid. "As to the accusations leveled against you, the way of it is clear enough. Five dead bodies. I accuse you of having a hand in that."

"Ah." Killian raised a brow. He prowled closer, his dark garb blending with the gloom, his bright gold hair the only light thing about him. There were grace and power in the way he moved, and suddenly, Sarah wished there was not. She wished he were ungainly and gangly. Less masculine. Less threatening.

Her gaze slid to the constables. All of a sudden, she saw Killian exactly as they must, as a powerful man who would surely emerge the victor in almost any altercation. All the more so if he chose to attack a sick and weakened patient.

He would never do that. She knew it. There was no question in her mind or in her heart.

Killian reached down and drew the sheet up, covering the face of the man in the bed, shielding him from dozens of eyes. "And when exactly did this patient expire?"

"Last night," snarled Mr. Simon. "I saw you here."

"Did you?" Killian did not appear particularly perturbed by the assertion, but Sarah noted the constables studying him with wary assessment. She edged closer and heard the one murmur to the other, "This man didn't die last night. The body lost its bladder and the sheets are still wet. I'd say the murder was closer to dawn, else the sheets would be dry or at the most, damp."

Sarah swallowed. Killian had left in the early hours of the morning, at the first light of dawn. She glanced at the sheet-draped body.

In time, an explanation of these repulsive acts would surely come to light, and that light would *not* shine on Killian Thayne.

But the constables did not know it, and they stepped toward him, flanking him on either side to block any possible escape.

"He's quite the bandy rooster, isn't he?" one asked with a nod at Mr. Simon. "All full of questions and knowing all the answers, yeah?"

Killian made no reply.

"Let's just step over here and have a brief chat, shall we?" said the other.

Killian walked with them to the side of the room.

Sarah followed, lifting soiled items from the floor as she went, hiding her interest behind the mundane task.

"So you were here the nights all five patients were killed. Can you tell us what you recall?" the dark-haired constable asked.

Killian looked around the ward. All eyes were trained upon them; all ears strained to hear. "May I suggest we adjourn to the corridor?" he said.

The constables agreed and the three of them stepped out.

Sarah lifted the water bucket, then wove her way between the beds, close enough to the open door to listen to what was said.

The dark-haired constable—she knew his voice now—repeated his questions. Killian replied with information both truthful and sparse, offering not a single word more than was absolutely required. As Sarah dipped the ladle and offered water to a patient, she realized that Killian never mentioned that he had seen her the night the woman had died in the sick ward. He never mentioned that she had been by Mr. Scully's bed, that she had seen a shadow. He never mentioned her at all. He kept her out of it.

The constables let him talk, listening, not interrupting.

When he was done, the second constable asked, "So that patient, Mr. Scully...he asked you to kill him? Did you do it out of pity? Is that what made you kill him?"

Sarah bit back a gasp and took a half-step forward before she could stop herself.

"I believe Mr. Scully's exact words were, '"Kill me and be done with it. You know the way of it, Mr. Thayne,"'" Killian said.

The dark-haired constable said, "So you killed him."

"No."

"When you killed him, did you think it an act of mercy?" the second constable asked.

"I did not kill him."

Sarah tightened her grip on the bucket handle as the constable threw another question at Killian and another, his colleague chiming in, until the drone of their voices buzzed as they challenged and prodded. Killian answered each sally with calm equanimity.

Sarah noticed they asked the same question again and again in different ways. *Were you with Mr. Scully when he died? So, what did you do for Mr. Scully at the moment he expired? When Mr. Scully died, how was he positioned in the bed? On his side? On his back?* They were not merely questions; they were thinly veiled accusations.

Though Killian remained calm, they were increasingly disinclined to believe his replies. Their doubt was evident in the tone of their voices and the cadence of the questions that came faster and harsher now.

For the third time, one of the constables asked him, "And exactly where were you at midnight last night, Mr. Thayne?"

For the third time, he answered, "Occupied elsewhere."

He sounded amused, and Sarah thought his attitude only further inflamed the officers, inclining them to believe the worst of him. She set down the bucket and glanced around to make certain that no one watched, then she edged forward so she stood at the open door and had a clear view of the three men. The constables stood side-by-side, facing away from her. Killian faced them, which meant he saw her there in the doorway. He offered no recognition of her presence in expression or action.

"And this morning? At dawn? Where were you then?"

"Occupied elsewhere."

"I am afraid that will not do, sir. I need details of your where-abouts, and witnesses who can attest to your activities during the time in question."

Sarah held her breath, her throat tightening, horror and fear congealing in a sickening knot. They believed that he had done this thing. They were convinced that he had killed this man in a hideous, unthinkable manner. No, not just *this* man. Many people. They thought Killian was responsible for all the questionable deaths on the wards.

Her first thought was for him. Her second was for herself. If he told them where he had been last night, what little security she had would be sliced away like a scalpel slicing away skin and muscle. If he said he had been with her, her position at King's College would be forfeit. What would happen to her then? She had managed to scrape aside two pounds four shillings in savings that she kept in a tin beneath the foot of her mattress. That money would not last her long if she found herself without employment.

She wet her lips, trying to think, to plan, to see a way clear of this disaster.

Killian's gaze met hers, and he made a small jerking movement of his head, as though willing her to leave. She understood then that he meant to protect her, even to his own detriment.

"I must insist that you accompany us to the station, where we can finish this discussion in a more appropriate venue," said the dark-haired constable as he exchanged a quick look with his companion.

Sarah clasped her hands before her to stop them trembling. She had heard about the interrogation rooms beneath the offices at Bow Street, heard about fists and cudgels and the manner in which suspects were *encouraged* to answer questions and admit their guilt. Anyone who lived in this parish had heard the horrible tales. But these were not

Bow Street Runners. They were constables of the Metropolitan Force. Would their methods be different? The thought that they might carry out such brutality on Killian, the image of him beaten and bloodied, made her ill.

One of the constables grabbed Killian's arm.

Behind her, the hubbub in the ward grew, closing in on her, a cacophony of sound.

She took a step back, thinking that she must flee. She turned and saw Mr. Simon's face and Mr. Franks', the apprentices', the patients'. Elinor stood to one side, her expression pinched with worry. Matron stood a few feet away, having come along the corridor and heard the last of the constable's words. Her lips were pressed in a taut line. She looked angry and disapproving, but when she stepped forward and said, "You err, sirs. I do not believe Mr. Thayne capable of such vile acts," no one paid her any mind.

Killian glanced down at the constable's hand on his arm, then lifted his gaze to Sarah.

They were going to do this. They were going to drag Killian away and see him charged with murder. Murders. Five murders.

Before she could ponder ramifications and consequences, Sarah stepped forward and said, "He was with me. I am your witness. He was with me—" her chin came up, and she finished firmly "—all night."

Killian swung his gaze to her, pewter and ice, and she read his shock that she spoke in his defense.

"He was with me," she said again, louder, firmer. "So he could not have killed anyone because he accompanied me to my lodging and remained there with me from ten o'clock last night until dawn."

Gasps and murmurs followed her words, and then silence.

Censure and condemnation hung in the air like a foul smell.

Of course, she had known it would be so even before she spoke. In saving Killian Thayne, she had doomed herself. A woman of loose moral character was not a woman to be respected and offered the opportunity of advancement on the wards.

Once before, the day Mr. Scully died, she had stepped forward in Killian's defense. That day, he had saved her from herself. But today, she was not so lucky, for so speedily had she forged into battle, there had not been a moment for her protector to stand before her.

"You assert that Mr. Thayne was with you the entire night?" the constable demanded.

"I do," she replied.

"The *entire* night?" The second constable stepped between her and Killian, using his physical presence to sever any influence that proximity might have over her answer.

She held his gaze and waited for uncertainty to creep to the fore on little rat feet. In truth, she could *not* swear that Killian had sat in the chair every moment of the night, guarding her door while she slept. He had been gone when she awakened, and he could have left at any time after she closed her door and locked it.

She looked back over her shoulder to the dead man on the bed. This time, the killer had ripped open the victim's throat. And still, there was not a drop of blood spilled.

I hear your blood rushing in your veins, Sarah. Killian's words echoed in her thoughts. How could he possibly hear her blood? How? And why had he said such a thing at all? *I am not like other men.*

His own softly spoken admissions were rife with macabre possibilities.

With a shudder, she looked away from the corpse, her gaze lifting to meet Killian's over the constable's shoulder.

The silence hung heavy, like a thick, cloying fog.

"Miss Lowell," Killian said, his attention focused on her, and she knew he meant to say more, to sacrifice himself for her honor, to ensure that her name not be besmirched by her assertion that he had remained at her side the night through.

"Killian Thayne never left my side during the hours between ten o'clock and dawn," she said again, her tone steady and sure. She *knew* it for the truth. He had told her he would guard her and keep her safe, and he had meant it. Whatever beast lurked beneath Killian's skin, it was not a beast that had done this murder.

She turned her attention fully on the dark-haired constable and stared him down, though her legs trembled beneath her skirt, and her pulse pounded so heavy and fast it made her temples throb. She must find a way to make these men understand that they were looking for their monster in the wrong place.

"He is not your killer, regardless of what Mr. Simon believes he saw. In fact, Mr. Simon—" she turned her head toward the man in question and found him watching her with narrow-eyed rage "—I believe you said that you saw the patient alive some time close to midnight, a full two hours after Mr. Thayne left King's College. With me."

She knew what they thought. That she had lain with Killian. That she had allowed him liberties of a base nature.

She almost laughed. If she was to be painted with that scarlet brush, she wished she had at least done something to deserve it.

Killian inclined his head, a spare movement, almost as spare as the tiny smile he offered her. He had not expected her defense of him. But he appreciated it. Appreciated *her*.

In that instant, she wanted to stride to his side, take his hand between her own and decry the constables' vile suspicions.

In that instant, she wished she were guilty of all the lascivious acts they suspected. She wished that she *had* allowed Killian those liberties, that she deserved the horrified looks the nurses and the matron cast her way.

The truth was, she might well have allowed them if he had only asked.

Because...Oh, sweet heaven...her heart twisted and she felt the blood drain from her cheeks. She was in love with him.

The magnitude of that realization left her reeling.

She thought she must have loved him for a very long time. For all the small kindnesses he offered to those less fortunate. For the way he offered each patient his undivided attention. For the way he spoke to her and listened to her and valued her words. For the way he had sat outside her door, his presence lessening her fear.

She was in love with Killian, despite—*and because of*—all his secret layers and hidden depths, all the mysteries and shadows that dogged him.

She was in love with a man they suspected of murder.

❧ 15 ❧

Paris, France, 1670

KILLIAN HAD BEEN BACK IN PARIS ONLY THREE WEEKS, AND HE FOUND *the streets and alleys to be both familiar and foreign. When last he visited, some sixty years earlier, he had been able to stroll from the north end of the city to the south at a leisurely pace and still arrive at his destination in under an hour. That Paris was gone, replaced by a city more than double in size. The population had doubled in size as well, a happy circumstance for one such as he.*

The fledgling night was cool and brisk, stars blinking overhead, a thin crescent moon bright against the dark sky. Killian walked along rue Neuve-Saint-Saveur, then down a long, uneven slope through the Courtyard of Miracles, home to all manner of criminals and thieves. He was quite certain he could find what he needed here.

The houses here were crumbling with age, families living one atop the next in poverty and crime—thieves passing their profession from parent to child. It was a place where he could hunt. He rounded one house, the walls half-fallen, and the hairs at his nape prickled and rose. He stilled, glanced back, but saw nothing.

No matter.

His senses might lie. They might be fooled.

But his instinct was that of a nocturnal beast, a monster, a killer, and that instinct was ever true.

Someone followed him. Not human. Someone like him.

Something primitive inside him recognized another monster, though in all the years he had never encountered one save his maker. He was torn by an instinct that demanded he terminate the interloper and the intellectual excitement of having the opportunity to discuss all manner of things with another like himself.

He kept his stride even and sure, his posture relaxed. Instinct bid him stop, turn, fight, kill the threat, rip it limb from bloody limb. Logic bid him be cautious, be stealthy. Be smart.

He picked up his pace only slightly as he rounded a corner, then ducked down a dark alley, turning to follow another and another, glad this part of the city had changed little since his last visit. In the end, he was behind his pursuer, prey no longer.

He caught a glimpse of a woman walking just ahead.

She was small and delicate, her blond hair piled atop her head in an intricate style, her gown flawless, diamonds at her throat.

Her shoulders stiffened. She turned her head to the right, not quite looking over her shoulder, certainly not meeting his gaze, but he knew she was aware of his presence. She knew he was there.

She faced forward once more and walked, and he followed.

She passed beneath an archway and he walked the same path seconds later, only to emerge on the far side and find the road empty. She was not there.

He started to turn, his movement aborted as a blow of unsurpassed power landed between his shoulder blades, throwing him forward against the wall. He pushed off, spun, and found the road empty still.

For a moment, he was disoriented, trying to make sense of the unexpected attack. He was strong, not in the way of a man, but in the way of a monster that was more than man. His adversary was stronger.

He spun and she closed her hand around his throat. She stared at him, then let him go and stepped back. He vibrated with the need to lunge at her and tear her throat out, to dismantle her body, to—

He mastered the urge; it made little sense. Here was a woman who was one of his kind, the first he had met in hundreds of years of roaming. He had ques-

tions. *Surely she had answers. Yet, beneath his skin, the primitive need to battle one who encroached on his territory screamed through his veins and made his muscles clench.*

"You surprise me," she said. "Only the very old can manage to stand this close and not bare their teeth and posture and growl. Yet, here you are, watching me, studying me...somehow mastering the need."

Killian clenched his jaw against the need to bare his teeth and posture and growl.

After a long pause, he said, "You are mastering the need, as well."

She laughed, a light, tinkling sound. "I have been vampire for over a thousand years. Age makes me wise and cautious—" her lashes swept low "—and able to control myself." She raised her gaze and met his own. "But you...you are able to do what most your age cannot. You are able to use intellect to master instinct."

Barely, but he did not say so. Instead, he said, "Why does instinct urge me to mark my territory, to chase you off or kill you?" Even saying the words out loud made a surge of territorial rage swell. He thought of the knowledge this creature surely possessed and held that thought as a way to control the animal need that clawed at him as surely as the hunger ever had. She had walked the Earth for more than a millennium. There was much she could tell him.

"We are predators," she said, moving her hand to encompass their surroundings. "Predators feed on the prey at hand. There is only so much prey available, and we are a territorial lot, guarding our sustenance. Did your maker not teach you?"

"How could he teach me? Would he not succumb to the urge to kill me?"

"A maker and his progeny are not subject to the territorial instinct. They can live together, hunt together, be together. It is the only chance for long term companionship for our kind." She sounded sad as she said the last and Killian wondered if she had made a companion, if her efforts had been successful. His one attempt certainly had not.

"My maker turned me and walked into the sun," he said.

Her eyes widened a fraction. "It surprises me that you survived."

"In the beginning, I surprised myself." He paused. "I have questions."

She nodded and reached for the ornate necklace at her throat. With a twist of her wrist, she freed what appeared to be a tiny dagger. She used it to nick her wrist.

Killian stared at the blood.

She laughed, low and throaty, then put her wrist to his lips. "Sip lightly, friend. It will quell the urge to kill me for a time."

He did as she bid, her blood strange in his mouth. It neither slaked nor stoked his hunger, but the taste was familiar. It tasted like the monster's blood that had made him.

She pulled her wrist away.

"Come," she said. "We will feed and then we will talk and then we will go our separate ways."

16

The dark-haired constable turned to Mr. Simon and asked, "Is there a place we can have this discussion without an audience?"

Mr. Simon bade the matron take them to his office whereupon began an interplay that Sarah might have found comedic were her nerves not drawn so taut. Mr. Thayne gestured for the constables to precede him, and they gestured for him to precede them, and then the dark-haired one gestured for the bewhiskered red-haired constable to go first. He demurred and then took a step forward, only to tread on his companion's foot as he, too, took a step.

Sarah caught Killian's eye. He lifted his brows but made no comment.

Finally, the dark-haired constable followed the matron with Killian behind him. Sarah made to follow, but the red-haired constable stopped her. He drew her off to one side and asked her to repeat again her assertions as to Killian's whereabouts the previous night. There was a shrewdness in his gaze that made Sarah think that the entire bumbling episode had been performed with the intent of creating in her a false sense of ease.

She was most definitely not at ease.

The constable asked her again about Killian's whereabouts, the question worded in a different manner, a challenge to the veracity of her words. She sighed and answered him, keeping every response to a single word if possible, a handful of words at most. And she did not alter her account, though the constable's mien went from shrewd to combative to leering. His questions grew increasingly more personal, his tone increasingly more aggressive.

When it was done and over with more than an hour had passed, and she was left standing alone in the hallway. She took a moment to gather herself and then walked into the ward intent on resuming her duties.

There, with sneering antipathy, Mr. Simon confronted her before all and dismissed her from her post.

"You are no longer employed at King's College," he said. "You will receive no recommendation from anyone at this hospital. Your conduct is unbecoming and reprehensible. You will leave the premises immediately."

She had expected exactly this, yet it still hurt.

She looked neither right nor left as she walked from the ward into the corridor. She had taken only a handful of steps when someone caught her hand. Elinor stood at her side.

"If you need me," she said, "come to the front doors at end of shift. Wait for me outside. Or come in the morning before shift. I don't have much, but what I have I'm happy to share."

Sarah blinked against the tears that pricked her lids. She wrapped her arms around Elinor's shoulders for a quick hug and dredged up a smile meant to reassure. "I'll be fine. You'd best get back before they decide to dismiss you as well just for speaking with me."

Elinor's face took on a mutinous expression, but Sarah refused to let her friend say or do anything rash on her account. "Go on. I will be fine, I promise."

She watched Elinor walk back into the ward then went and gathered her cloak and left the building.

A thick fog had rolled in, heavy and damp. Caught in the gray blanket of cloying mist that clung to her skin and obscured the way, she could see little of what lay ahead.

Footsteps sounded from behind her, heavy and quick.

She turned but could see little more than a tall form in a dark overgarment. Of King's College, there was no sign; the fog had swallowed it whole. She backed up several steps, then lifted her hem, preparing to flee, but a voice hard and angry called out, "Miss Lowell."

She froze. The voice was vaguely familiar. "Miss Lowell," he said again, as though he knew she was nearby, but could see her no better than she could see him.

The form stepped forward to reveal a long black coat, black-gloved hands, and a black top hat.

With a gasp, she fell back another step.

Her pursuer lifted his head and she gasped again when she recognized one of the apprentices from the hospital, Mr. Watts.

For an instant, she couldn't move, couldn't think, fear icing her mind, her limbs.

Then anger crept in, and with it, the recollection that she was not helpless. She was armed. She was prepared.

"Why are you following me, Mr. Watts?" she demanded, surreptitiously pulling her cudgel free of her cloak.

She glared at him, studying his expression, his posture, watching for any clue that he might attack. Something nagged at her. Something not quite right...

He glared back. "I have words I need to say to you."

"Words? You could have spoken to me at the hospital. At any point over these many months, you could have spoken to me. Instead, you chose to follow me, terrorize me, steal into my home in the darkness—"

"What? No—" All anger drained from his face, replaced by confusion. "I never did that."

"Never followed me? Your presence belies that claim."

"No, I did follow you, but... I mean—" He shook his head. "I have followed you twice. Just now, and last night. Not over the course of months. And I never terrorized you."

Sarah kept her cudgel at the ready. "Last night you stole into my chamber when I was not there and then stalked me through St. Giles, called my name, chased me through the alleys."

Mr. Watts lifted his gloved hands before him, palms forward. "I did not." He shook his head. "I most certainly did not. I saw you walking on Great Russel Street last night. You were brisk, almost at a run. I was concerned so I followed."

"That is a lie," Sarah said. She could read it in his expression.

He sighed. "I did see you on the street. But I did not follow out of concern. I followed because I finally worked up the courage to tell you..." Whatever courage he had possessed last night failed him now, because his voice trailed away and he did not confide what it was that had driven him to seek her out last night.

His hands dropped to his sides and his expression darkened. "I saw you with him. Mr. Thayne. I watched you. I saw you lead him inside." He paused. "I thought you were a different sort. I thought you...me... we..." His lips formed a bitter twist. "I was mistaken. I was there this morning when you made your sordid admission. You are not the woman I imagined you to be." The last was said with a mixture of accusation and derision.

His explanation took a moment to become clear in her thoughts, and when it did, she was both startled and dismayed. "You mean to say that you built a dream of—" she gestured back and forth between them "—some sort of intimacy between us. Without ever having so much as a conversation with me? And now you are angry in your newfound realization that no such intimacy exists? That I am not the image you created in your secret fancy?" She drew herself up. "How dare you? How dare you follow me now to berate me in this manner? You have no say over my actions."

At her words, Mr. Watts deflated, his shoulders slumping, his head hanging forward. He pulled his hat from his head and turned it in his hands, over and over. She stared at the hat in his hands and realized what it was that had nagged at her when he first emerged from the mist. The hat was wrong, a top hat, whereas her pursuer the previous evening had worn a low crowned hat. Too, as she looked at him now, she realized that while Mr. Watts was tall, he was not broad enough and he carried himself like a boy inhabiting the body of a man.

He spoke the truth.

He was not the man who had stalked her all these months.

Sarah turned away. "Go back to the hospital," she said. "We have no further words that need be exchanged."

He called after her but she walked on, past the graveyard, the stones obscured from view under their blanket of fog. She did not look back, but she knew he did not follow.

She reached Coptic Street without further incident. Sounds echoed around her, the distant creak of a wheel, the jingle of a bridle, but the coach in possession of both was veiled from sight. It was eerie and unsettling; the entire world had been swallowed by the fog.

Continuing on, she passed a mangy dog that sniffed at the gutter, then she jerked to a stop as Mrs. Cowden's house materialized from the mist, ghostly tendrils wrapping around the crumbling chimney. The sight of the house, dark and shabby, drove deep the vile desperation of her circumstances.

Tears pricked her lids, and she dashed them away with the back of her hand. There was no value in tears of frustration and anger, fear and hopelessness. They would only serve to leave her nose red and her lids puffy.

They would neither change nor solve anything.

In the end, she would still have only days left until her rent was due once more, and though her savings might stretch to pay it, they would not stretch for long.

In the end, she would still be without employment or reference.

In the end, her good name would still be besmirched by her own words.

And in the end, she would still be in love with Killian Thayne.

Her situation was fraught with the greatest uncertainty.

Her options at the moment were so narrow and frayed, she was having a difficult time seeing them at all. And despite that, she knew that if faced with the same choice in the same setting, she would again do exactly as she had done. Because she could not let them take him.

The sound of wheels clacking on the cobblestones and the clopping of horses' hooves made her head jerk up and her gaze dart along the street. As though teased apart with the tip of a knife, the fog parted to reveal four great black beasts and, behind them, a gleaming black coach. Instinctively, she stepped back, only to find the carriage rocking to a halt several paces away, directly in front of Mrs. Cowden's lodging house.

This was a private coach, a rich man's coach.

A prickling sense of expectation bloomed, for she had no doubt as to the owner of the carriage. She had known by his dress and his mode of speech that surely Killian was from a different world than the other surgeons at King's College—a different world even than the comfortable one she had been raised in. But this coach, with its gleaming finish and beautifully matched horses, spoke of wealth beyond what she could have imagined.

The sight of it was both welcome and worrisome, for Killian's presence here created a labyrinth of complexities and enticements.

A footman climbed down and stood by the carriage door. He wore a smart green and gold livery, as did the coachman on the bench.

Feeling as though she slogged through a bog that mired her every step, Sarah walked the last dozen paces to the coach. As she stopped beside the footman, the clouds above parted to let a single beam of light fall upon her, sending the shadow of the carriage stretching along the cobblestones.

The footman glanced at the light and frowned. "This way, miss," he said, indicating the door on the far side, away from the light.

Wary of the horses that snorted and pawed the ground, she offered them a wide berth as she rounded the carriage. The footman opened the door. She blinked and peered into the dim confines. Killian sat in the far corner, wrapped in shadow and mystery.

The collar of his cloak was raised high, and his hands were gloved in black leather. She frowned, certain there was some significance to that, but unable to place exactly what.

"Come inside please, Sarah," he said. "I wish to speak with you."

A request? An order? She could not say. But since she had much she wished to ask him, much she wished to say, she took the footman's offered hand and allowed him to help her inside the coach.

Settling herself in the corner opposite Killian, as far from him as the small space would allow, she waited in silence as the footman closed the door, leaving them alone. She could see only the hint of highlight on Killian's brow, his nose, his chin. The blinds were pulled down over the windows. Wishing to have a clear perspective of his expression, Sarah reached to raise one and let in what little light had penetrated through cloud and mist.

Killian moved quickly, leaning forward to trap her wrist. He tipped his head down and looked at her over the rim of his dark spectacles, his gaze intent, and she thought she ought to be afraid. But she was not. For some inexplicable reason, when she was with Killian, she felt safer, more secure, more confident than she ever had in her entire life. She felt as though he opened a dam and let her soul dance free, let her be exactly who she was.

Strange thoughts. Mad thoughts.

"Leave the blind," he said softly. "The light is too bright."

She thought he spoke in jest, but a glance disabused her of that notion. He found even this fog-shrouded day too bright for his comfort.

For a flickering instant, she had the terrible thought that he was as her father had been, an opium addict whose eyes were pained by even modest illumination. Yet, Killian evinced none of the traits associated with that malady. Her father had been lethargic, his pupils ever constricted, his speech slurred. He had shown no interest in his appearance or grooming. In the end, she had barely known him, for his mannerisms and behavior were so drastically altered.

By contrast, Killian was alert, his clothing impeccable, his intellect sharp and clear.

Perhaps he simply disliked the sun. Perhaps. But wariness unfurled inside her.

"Are you cold?" he asked, cutting the silence.

It was only then that she realized she was trembling.

He did not wait for her answer, but loosened his hold on her wrist and spread a thick blanket over her legs, then used the toe of his boot to push a warming brick along the floor. "Drape the blanket over top and the heat will rise to warm you."

"Thank you," she murmured, touched by his consideration. Then, "Why do you have the brick? You said you do not feel the cold."

"You remember that, do you?" He paused. "I do not notice the cold. I brought the brick for you."

He settled back in the corner and studied her for a moment, leaving her strangely uncomfortable and disconcerted.

But no longer cold.

"It seems you are ever leaping to my defense, Sarah." He dipped his head, toyed with the edge of his glove, then looked up once more, his expression unreadable. "Why did you lie for me?"

"Did I lie?" she asked. "Did you leave your place at my door and return to the hospital sometime before dawn?" She did not believe he had, and that made her either very intuitive or very foolish.

He smiled a little. "No. I never left."

"Then I did not lie. I merely reworded the truth. You did accompany me into my lodging and remained there with me from ten o'clock last night until dawn. The fact that there was a door between us is irrelevant."

He reached over and ran the backs of his gloved fingers along her cheek. She had to force herself to sit still, to refrain from leaning into his touch. "Why did you sacrifice yourself for me?" The regret and pain in his tone tugged at her heart.

"They were going to take you," she said, her voice low. She dropped her gaze to the tips of his perfectly polished boots. "The constables. They were going to take you to the interrogation rooms. I have heard what they do in the rooms below Bow Street. Everyone has. I cannot imagine the Metropolitan Police rooms are very different. They would have hurt you." The thought of that horrified her. "They would have beaten you, left you bloodied and bruised."

"Bruises heal," he said.

"I could not bear it if they hurt you." She raised her head and saw that he watched her with complete attention, his expression one of bemused wonder.

"I would rather they hurt me than for any harm to befall you," he said. "I wish to see you safe, Sarah. Safe and protected. Free to live a wonderful life."

A bark of laughter escaped her. "Wonderful?" She shook her head. "My life is wonderful in some ways. Not in others." She paused. "You say you want me safe and protected. Then you must understand why I could not let them hurt you. And they would have...to make you confess to crimes you did not commit. They would have beaten you, broken your surgeon's hands..."

He caught her hand and lined it up with his, palm to palm, fingers to fingers. He closed his eyes as though savoring the contact even through his glove and hers. "And you know with certainty that I did not commit these crimes?" He opened his eyes.

"I do." She nodded, feeling fierce and certain. "I know you could never do that, never harm someone weak and ill."

He appeared taken off guard by her ferocity.

"Do not paint me with gilded righteousness, Sarah." Sadness flickered across his features. "There are things you do *not* know of me. Things I did many, many years ago when I was a different creature than I am today."

"Creature?" She let her fingers slide between his and curled them over, holding on. "You say the word as though you are some ravening beast. You are not. You are a man."

Leaning forward to rest one elbow on his knee, he lifted her free hand and pressed his lips against the backs of her knuckles.

Oh, the sweet sensation of his touch. It poured through her like rich, red wine. She read such longing in him, such pain, as though he was desperate for this contact. As desperate as she.

She ached for him to kiss her and hold her so tight against him that she could feel his heart beat.

"I am many things, Sarah. I have been many things." He was mere inches away. Her breath locked in her throat and her pulse galloped.

"Whatever you have been, whatever you are, I know you, Killian. I *know* you."

"You do not." And he sounded inordinately sad as he said it. He said nothing more for a moment, then spoke, very softly. "I wanted to grab him by the throat and slam him against the wall when I heard from Mrs. Bayley that he had censured you. Demeaned you."

Mr. Simon. He spoke of Mr. Simon, who had sneered at her after the constables had finished questioning her. He had not even offered her the respect of privacy when he had dismissed her from King's College, impugned her integrity, looked at her as though she were refuse to be scraped off his boot. He had dismissed her in front of everyone. It was a humiliation that scored deep.

"If you felt dismay on my behalf, then you must understand the dismay I felt on yours. You understand why I could not let the constables take you, impugn you, accuse you of horrific crimes." She cocked her head. "It is better that you did not grab Mr. Simon by the throat. Whatever he is or is not, the patients derive some benefit from his care."

"It was only the realization that such actions would render your sacrifice meaningless that held me in check. That, and the desire to deserve the gilded halo you attribute to me." This last was said with a sardonic edge.

Sarah could summon no reply, and so they sat for a moment in silence while she tried to gather her thoughts and emotions into some semblance of calm. Her world was coming unraveled at the seams, and she was not certain how to drag the edges back together.

Killian made a vague gesture toward the closed door of the carriage. "Would you prefer to wait while I have Jones pack for you, or shall we proceed now and I can send someone to fetch your belongings later?"

"Pack? I don't..." *I don't understand.* But she did. Killian meant to take her away from here. To bring her...where?

He lifted something from the seat beside him and extended his hand. She saw then that he held the pretty porcelain saucer that had been hers since childhood.

"You were in my room," she said. "How? I locked it this morning."

"And the women who live in the room next to you have a key."

She frowned. "They let you in?"

"They were in there already. They said you pay them for laundry services."

"I do." Her chin came up. "Even with what little coin I have, that expense was justified. It is—was—important for me to look presentable at the hospital and my schedule did not allow for washing garments with the frequency my position required." She paused. "But that does not explain why they let you in."

He smiled, a flash of teeth, the hint of a dimple. "I can be most persuasive when the matter is of import."

"You consider me a *matter?*" she asked.

"I consider you of import," Killian replied, his expression solemn now.

Sarah dropped her gaze and took the dish from him to cup it in her palms. ""How did you know that I would want this? Of all the things in my chamber, this is the one that means something to me."

"I know much about you, Sarah. I know every subtle glance, the way you breathe, the delicate sweep of your lashes. I know the tilt of your head and the pull of your lips when you are puzzling out a solution. I know the set of your shoulders and the curve of your back. You are endlessly fascinating to me." He gestured at the dish. "I noted your expression when you looked at it last night. I could see it meant something to you."

His words made her heart race, and she had no need to wonder if he knew it, because he said, "I can hear each precious pulse, Sarah, feel each beat of your heart."

Impossible. Surely he could not. But somehow she believed him. Believed he did feel her, hear her. Believed he *knew* her.

She turned her head away, staring at the lowered blind, imagining the street beyond. As the fog outside obscured the street, so too was her future obscured. She could not see the path that would carry her into tomorrow, and next week, and next month. But she knew that wherever that path might lead, she had the opportunity now to be with Killian, to snatch moments of happiness. And she *would* snatch them. Finally, she said, "Where do we go?"

"We go home. My home, now yours." And all the arguments that tumbled to her lips died as he turned his gaze upon her. "I offer you the world, Sarah. Anything you want."

She believed him in that as well. "What do you demand in return?"

"Demand? No, I only ask. I ask for you. Your company. Your smile. Your eyes, dancing and pleased as they look to mine. Your intellect. Your valor. But mind me well, Sarah, you will need that valor. I am not an easy...man."

The hesitation hung in the air, a warning, but not a surprise. She had seen from the start that he had depths like a roiling ocean in the midst of a storm. She sensed he meant it as a warning of something deeper, something greater. But he was not ready to tell her. Not yet.

He shared something of import here, some secret that shimmered between them and slid away from her like smoke. She tried to clasp it, to see it clearly, but the meaning dissipated, and she was left with the certainty that his words revealed something she did not quite grasp.

"Well, I suppose that I am neither meek nor submissive, which makes me a somewhat difficult woman, wouldn't you say?"

He made a soft laugh, his eyes glittering in the dim light. "I would have you only as you are, and no other way. The thought of having you by my side, of sharing the world with you is a heady temptation." His tone turned muted and dark, his eyes bleak. "I have been alone for a very long while."

"I understand loneliness," she whispered.

Again, that fleeting, dark smile, as though her words both amused and saddened him.

He reached down and lifted something else from the seat. The yellowed magazine that held the story her father had found so fascinating. Polidori's *The Vampyre.*

Offering it to her, he held her gaze, and she sensed that unlike her candle dish, he had not retrieved this out of care and kindness, but for another reason entirely. Cautious and watchful, she took the pages from him, her pulse speeding up, her thoughts tumbling to and fro as a strange expectation suffused her.

I am not an easy...man.

I have been alone for a very long while.

You have not read Byron's The Giaour?... *It is a poem about a monster damned to drain life from those it loves.*

Something clicked inside her, a key in a lock.

No. What was she thinking? It was not possible.

The Vampyre.

The smoky ideas that had eluded her a moment past coalesced, and she was left speechless and overwhelmed.

Impossible. And...not. It explained so much.

He stared at her, unsmiling, severe. She had the thought that he knew the direction her suppositions traveled. That he *wanted* them to flow toward that impossible conclusion.

Her breath stuttered to a stop, trapped in her lungs, and she stared at him, suddenly certain. Certain of the impossible, the terrible, the mad.

Inexorably drawn, her gaze dipped to the magazine once more. The seconds ticked past, protracted and sluggish.

"You did not kill those people at King's College," she whispered, the words so soft she wondered that he could hear her at all. When he made no reply, she raised her head and realized that he waited only for that, that he wanted her to look at him as he made his response.

"No, I did not kill them." His eyes, liquid mercury, gleamed in the dim light, boring deep inside her.

"But you could have." She wrapped her arms around her waist and held herself tight. "You could have because..."

There was both sorrow and resignation etched on his face as he finished the thought that she dared not speak aloud. "Because I am—" He paused, and she waited, her breath stalled in her chest, then he shook his head and finished, "I am not like other men."

And suddenly, that assertion was laced with a multitude of subtle inferences and implications that she was not yet ready to drag into the light.

In that moment, though she knew not its source, she felt his suffering as her own.

Whatever his tormented secrets, she recognized in him like to like, knew that whatever horrors he had known and seen, whatever mysteries lurked in his heart, he was even more alone than she.

That he needed her as she needed him.

17

At Killian's instruction, the coach set off. He closed his eyes and rested his head back against the velvet squabs, baring the strong column of his throat. Once, Sarah stretched out her hand, almost brave enough to lay her fingers against his neck and feel the steady, solid throb of the pulse that beat beneath his skin. In the end, she dropped her hand and contented herself with letting her gaze roam his features. Her heart swelled with the knowledge that he had come for her.

He had cared enough to come for her.

She concentrated on the wonder of that rather than the multitude of questions that their cryptic dialogue had skirted.

Mindful of the light, she leaned close to the window and peeked through the lifted edge of the blind as the carriage rocked to a halt before Killian's town home in Berkeley Square. His was the last house in a row of very large, very tall houses. There was a black ironwork fence surrounding the entirety, with a break at the stairs that ascended to the front door, and another that descended to the servants' entry.

Sarah counted four floors, each with three large rectangular windows across the front, save for the ground floor, which had two windows to the left of the front door.

After a moment, the liveried footman opened the carriage door and waited as Sarah gathered her candle dish and the magazine. She caught her lower lip between her teeth, staring at the curled and faded pages...wondering...

Raising her gaze, she found Killian watching her, his expression bland and cool.

She turned away, and let the footman hand her down from the coach. Killian descended behind her. She glanced back to see that he had put his spectacles in place to shade his eyes. He kept his head bowed, his thick, honey gold hair falling forward to veil his features.

Without a word, he offered his arm, and she sensed that any questions she had would be better spoken indoors rather than out here, for it was clear that even this dim, cloud-filtered light was uncomfortable for him.

They ascended the stairs and he did not wait for a butler or maid to open the door, but opened it himself and gestured for Sarah to precede him inside. The hallway was dark but beautiful. Paneled walls of rich gleaming wood. A semi-circular console table just inside the entry with a vase of deep red roses. There was thought and artistry in the presentation.

The scent of beeswax left a faint signature in the air, topped by the breath of the roses. Killian drew off his gloves and tossed them on the table, then swung his cloak from about his broad shoulders and handed it to a maid who stepped forward and curtsied before taking the garment from his hands.

Sarah caught her breath as Killian stepped around behind her to stand close at her back. His breath fanned her neck, sending shivers of awareness dancing across her skin.

"May I?" he murmured, and she nodded, wordless. He took her cloak and passed it to the maid. And then they were alone. He radiated warmth. She could feel it through all the layers of her clothing and his. How long since she had been warm? Truly warm? Body, heart, and mind. She had been frozen for so long. Certainly, since her father had died, but at this moment, she thought she had been frozen even before that, her existence held within a rigid box that was imposed by her sex, by society, by expectations. Despite her father's nature, the fact that he had viewed her as an asset in his work and treated her not merely as a daughter, but as a person in her own right, she had been denied the opportunity to be all that she dreamed. She was grateful that her father had fed her curiosity, stimulated her mind. Even so, she had felt that she could only walk so far along the road before she met a solid gate that barred her passage.

She looked at Killian and asked, "Why?" He did not request clarification. He seemed to understand what she asked. *Why me? What is it that draws you?*

He removed his dark spectacles and looked down at her for a long moment, his expression solemn. Then he rested his palm on the top of her head. "Because your thoughts, your intellect, your dry wit appeal to me." He slid his hand lower and brushed the pad of his thumb along her lower lip. She caught her breath at the contact, struck by the urge to take his thumb in her mouth, to suck on it and taste his skin. "Because the things you say are interesting or funny or wise. Or simply soothing, the sound of your voice, the cadence of your speech." He stroked his fingertips along her throat, his gaze never leaving hers, then let them slide along her breastbone, and lower, to her waist, her hip. There, he stopped, resting his palm on the side of her hip so his long, strong fingers curved to follow the curve of her buttock. He leaned a little closer. "Because you are not fearless but brave. Because you have a moral core that guides your choices."

His pupils were dark, surrounded by a thin rim of gray.

Her breath came too fast, too shallow.

"Because," he said as he walked around her so he stood at her back and leaned close to speak against her ear, his hand sliding forward, his long fingers splayed across her belly. Society would have her protest, refuse his touch, but at this moment Sarah could not think of a single reason to heed society's norms and expectations. She liked the feel of his hands on her far too much.

"You make me feel things I had thought buried," he continued. She let her head tip back to rest against him. "I want to touch you, Sarah, caress you, make you cry out in pleasure. I want to coddle you and protect you, even as I want to set you free. I want to watch you fly. I want to give you the world."

With his hand curled around the back of her neck, he walked around so he faced her once more. "Have you been with a man?" he asked, his voice a low rasp.

Her voice was gone, stolen by the heat of his fingers on her skin and the look in his eyes. Her only answer was a shake of her head.

"I want you, Sarah," he said, his gaze never leaving hers. "I have wanted you from the moment I first saw you. I want to kiss you, taste you. I want you in my arms and underneath me in my bed. I want to fill your body and your thoughts. I want to hear you scream my name."

His words wound through her thoughts, making her see the picture he painted. Her breath came too fast, uneven. Her head spun. She wanted all he described. She wanted him.

She leaned toward him. It was enough. With a sound of pleasure, he pulled her against him, his mouth on hers, hard, demanding. His tongue slid past her lips and she opened in invitation, tasting him, teasing him. He moved his lips to her throat, his tongue tasting her skin, her pulse beating a wild and wicked tattoo.

And then he stepped away.

"What..." Sarah wet her lips.

"Choose," he said. "Choose while your thoughts are not muddled by my kisses. Choose to walk to your left and I will ring the maid to serve tea in the parlor."

"And my second choice?" she asked, still breathless.

Killian offered his hand, his lashes sweeping down to hide his eyes.

Take his hand and follow where he led. Take his hand and follow to a place where he would kiss her and taste her and make her scream his name.

She took his hand. His lashes swept up, his gaze triumphant and joyous.

Killian twined his fingers with hers and led her through the house, up carpeted stairs with banisters of gleaming polished wood, through hallways lit only by lamplight, the heavy draperies pulled across the windows.

At last, they reached a heavy double door, and he threw it open then drew her inside.

"My lair," he murmured, and a tickle of apprehension crawled through her at his choice of words.

She hesitated then stepped deeper into the chamber. The walls were covered in blue paper that had a subtle texture, like velvet. A thick, soft carpet of darker blue with a design of green and yellow birds covered the floor. There were two large chairs before the fireplace, each matched with a low footstool. A spacious room, handsome in appearance.

"You like fine things," she observed.

"I do."

"Yet you work in one of the poorest hospitals in the city."

An instant of silence. Then, "Because they do not have fine things. I dislike the imbalance."

She recalled the way he tucked shillings into the night nurse's apron and realized that she had already known this about him, though she had not defined it in such a pared down manner.

Her feelings for him bubbled to the surface, and she turned away lest he read them in her gaze. The feelings she had for him were too new, too raw. She was not ready to explain, perhaps to have them rebuffed. She did not think she could bear that.

Pressing her lips together, she shifted closer to the fireplace. Above the oaken mantelpiece was a large painting of a river. The dominant colors were blue and aqua and yellow and gold. She gazed up in mute wonder, drawn into the beauty and brightness of the watercolor.

"Turner," Killian murmured from behind her. "Some call him the painter of light."

It was true. The painting embodied light, captured it and set it free, pure and brilliant. And Killian hung it in his chamber, he who clung only to the shadows.

The thought made her sad.

He was not a creature of light. That much was clear.

"Do you long for it, for the sunlight? For the warmth of it on your skin?" She could not tear her eyes from the painting. She felt as though the sun's rays poured from the canvas to touch her face.

"No, I do not long for it. Not anymore. The moonlight has a cool and wonderful beauty, the night its own sweet music." He moved close behind her. She could feel the heat of him. "I remember the sunlight with a vague and hazy fondness, but I do not long for it. It was a small sacrifice in exchange for all I have gained. I have learned to love the night."

His words brought so many questions to her lips, questions she dared not ask for she was not yet certain what she would do with the answers. She closed her eyes, every sense tingling with awareness, with the knowledge that he was so close. All she had to do was reach out and she could know the answers to untold mysteries. About him. About herself.

If only she dared.

Dipping his head until his nose grazed the skin of her neck, he breathed in, his nearness and his action combining to set her heart racing. She ached for the stroke of his hand, the feel of his lips.

Closing her eyes, she leaned back a little into his embrace.

"Be certain, Sarah," he whispered against the side of her throat, sending a tinkling cascade dancing through her.

She knew all he meant with those softly voiced words. Be certain it was this she wanted, *him* she wanted. The unconventional life he offered. She did not know where he meant this to lead, but she could not imagine he offered her forever. She imagined he wanted her for his mistress for a time, and she refused to let societal judgment steal this joy. She would be his mistress and she would enjoy the moments they had together to the fullest.

"I am certain," she whispered. She had no wish to cling to her past, had no idea of her future. In this moment, she was changed from the woman she had always been. In this moment, she wanted only to *live,* to allow herself that luxury, that beauty. To know Killian's touch, to offer him her love, even if this day was all she ever had of him, all they ever shared.

Tomorrow would come regardless, and it would hold the same fears and uncertainties whether she indulged her heart or not. So, for one shining snippet of the unfurling ribbon that was her life, she would grab hold of what she wanted and take what she could.

Reaching up, she pulled the pins from her hair and let it fall about her shoulders and down her back.

"Your hair is beautiful, a sleek, dark curtain with just a whisper of wayward curl at the ends." He stroked his palm down the length, emphasizing his point. That touch made her mouth go dry and her pulse jerk like a skittish colt.

"You are beautiful, Sarah." His words and the rich, lovely cadence of his voice mesmerized her. "The pink flush of your skin—" he drew his thumb along the edge of her jaw "—the lush curve of your lips—" his fingers slid to her lips, rubbed and stroked, and as her mouth opened on a gasp, the tip of his index finger dipped inside "—you are so lovely to me."

On instinct, she licked his fingertip, then closed her teeth on him and bit down.

His sharp intake of breath stabbed through her, sinking to her breasts, her belly, her trembling legs. Because she knew she ignited him. There was a lush and heady pleasure in that.

"You bite," he murmured.

She hesitated but an instant, then whispered, "As, I suspect, do you." There. She had done it. Acknowledged the secret that hovered between them. On some level, she understood. And she knew that he would not hurt her.

He pulled her toward him then, taking her mouth in a hungry kiss, his tongue tasting her, his teeth nipping lightly at her lips. Pleasure spilled through her blood like a tide, making her breath rasp and her pulse race. Her skin felt too tight. Her clothes were unbearable fetters, and she hissed a sigh of relief as he began to loosen them. He slid each piece from her, kissing and caressing every inch of skin he bared. He ran his tongue along the top of her breast, and she arched her back, offering herself to him. She wanted the rest of her clothing gone. She wanted his mouth on her everywhere.

Modesty demanded she blush and protest. Desire demanded that she open her mouth and taste him as he tasted her. She twined her fingers in his hair and brought her mouth to his, certain that if she did not kiss him, she would not survive it. The flavor of his kiss was heady, more wonderful than the finest wine she had ever sampled.

The cool air in the room touched her, making her shiver. The sheets of his bed were even cooler as he guided her there and pressed her back against them, his fingers splayed lightly across her throat. She could feel her pulse drumming against his fingertips.

With a groan, he traced his tongue along her jaw, her throat, his mouth coming to lie against her pulse. He kissed her there, his mouth open, insistent. She arched her neck, the graze of his teeth making her gasp, sending spiraling tendrils of need winding through her veins.

Feeling weightless and dizzy and wonderfully alive, she lay back and watched as he dragged off his coat, then his shirt, pulling the cloth over his head and down his arms. He bared the wonderful mystery of his chest, covered in dark gold hair that tapered to a thin line down the middle of his taut belly. She had seen shirtless men before, but none had been Killian. She came up on her knees and traced the tips of two fingers along the ridges of muscle that formed his chest, his belly.

"You are lovely," she whispered. He was. But she had expected that, expected the lithe, lean lines and sculpted edges. She studied him in open curiosity, awed and amazed, and he laughed, a low wicked chuckle that stroked her senses.

His eyes never left hers as he prowled closer to rest his knee between her own on the mattress. He kissed her and eased her back so she lay beneath him.

Her body arched of its own accord, instinctively seeking his touch as he trailed his fingers down her neck, along her collar bone, to the swell of her breast above the thin cotton of her chemise. Feeling like a bow drawn taut, bent to its limit, she waited to see what he would do next.

A gasp escaped her, and it became a purr as he closed his hand about the soft flesh of her breast, stroked his thumb over her tight nipple through the thin cloth of her chemise. He lowered his head and closed his lips on her through the cloth, gentle suction that gave way to a more demanding pull. The sensation was like fire and ice and fireworks exploding in the sky, only the explosion was inside her, inside her blood, an aching need that spread. Heat. Liquid heat.

"Please." She knew not what she begged for. But he knew.

Reaching down, he closed his fists in her chemise and tore it open, baring her to his gaze, his touch. His features were hard, hungry, and the way he looked at her made an answering hunger rear inside her.

He let his weight down full upon her, wonderfully heavy, holding her and freeing her, the hard ridge of his arousal between her thighs. She had never felt anything more breathtaking, more sensual. Longing burgeoned and swelled, and she cried out as he closed his mouth again on her nipple, the erotic tug making her body squirm. Then he offered sweet kisses and gentle bites until she was panting and writhing beneath him.

Running her hands along his shoulders and down the hard planes of his chest, she explored the feel of his smooth skin, taut over lean layers of muscle. He was wonderfully masculine, wonderfully appealing.

His mouth moved again to her throat, his hands skimming her waist, and lower, dipping between her thighs to touch her sex. She felt swollen and tender and pliant and wet and when he touched her there, all those things combined into a tight, restless coil. She ached for his touch there, but his touch made her feel as though she needed to squirm and writhe. She moaned, lost in sensation.

She had never imagined this. Never. It was like a tempest inside her own body, a magnificent tempest that lured her to fling herself into the storm with untrammeled abandon.

Her body stirred, her hips rolling in a way she did not deliberately intend. But the movement felt so good, so right. She felt as though he led her to a place she had always known and never even thought to look for. Hot and quivering, sensation poured through her. She was alive, so alive.

Between her thighs, his arousal was thick and heavy, pressing against her sex. Again, her hips rocked up, and she felt a slick pressure, there, between her folds. The pressure became a burn, and the burn became pain. But before she could protest, he slid his hand between them and his fingers—those clever fingers—made her crave the burn, the pressure, the invasion. She opened to him, sliding her heels along the smooth, soft sheets, shifting to an angle that increased the incredible feelings he stirred.

Cupping her breast, he stroked her and rocked his hips to bring himself tighter against her. There was a tautness, a pressure as he pushed inside her a little more, and she gave a shocked cry at the intrusion, the foreign sensation of being stretched and entered.

He held himself back. She could feel that in the leashed tension of his body. A press; a release. Just a little of his erection easing in to fill and stretch. It was alien and frightening and beguiling all at once, and she could not help but catch his rhythm and move with him. Again and again until she was panting, half in apprehension, half in wild abandon.

What a mad slurry of feelings. She wanted him, ached for him, but could not help but be a little afraid of the unknown.

And then it was unknown no longer. He pushed harder, the stretching so powerful and strange, she cried out. A sharp instant of discomfort, a burning, an ache, and then he was inside her, deep inside her, fully sheathed.

She lay there panting, a little dismayed.

As though he knew everything she felt, he simply stayed as he was, allowed her to understand the feeling of his body joined with hers, and then he began to move, a shallow thrust, a retreat. She didn't dislike it, not precisely, but...

He slid his hand down her belly to her soft curls, to her slick folds and the place so sensitive it made her moan. He caressed her there with lazy swirls of his fingers until she gasped and arched up to meet each shallow thrust. Wanting more. Needing more. He moved faster now, and deeper, and while the pain was not completely gone, it wasn't precisely pain anymore. And as his fingers pressed harder and slid faster, she arched and dug her heels against the sheets, striving and failing to find that which she craved.

With a little cry, she reached down and locked her fingers around his wrist, holding his hand exactly where it was, aching for something she could not name.

Too much. It was all too much. She could not bear it, could not hold fast to the spiraling pieces of herself.

She twined her fingers through his hair as he thrust deep and hard, his breath ragged as he turned his face into the crook of her elbow.

Hot and sharp, she felt his bite, there on the soft skin at the inside of her elbow.

"Killian—" She cried out, and tried to make him understand, but it was too late. The sensation of his fingers sliding along her wet sex, and the feel of his penis moving inside her...She was flying apart, a thousand shining bits of her all flying apart.

And he was with her, flying with her, his release coming an instant after her own as he thrust deep one last time, throbbing inside her, spilling himself inside her.

She clung to him, floating, and finally drifting back to herself.

Panting, bewildered, wonderfully replete, she lay there and stared up at the gilded ceiling, one arm draped across Killian's broad back, the other flung free across the sheets.

He kissed her neck, her cheek, and finally roused himself to lift his weight from her and roll to the side. She missed it immediately. The weight of him. The heat.

She snuggled against him and smiled as he slid his arm around her and drew her close. Slowly, she lifted her lids, and languidly eased her arm across his chest.

Frowning, she stared at the golden expanse of his skin, and it took her a moment to understand what she saw.

Blood. She had left a smear of blood when she moved her arm over his skin.

She jerked to a sitting position and stared at the crook of her elbow. Her veins traced blue beneath her skin, and there were two small punctures there and a small smear of her blood.

He had bitten her. Tasted her. The thought was both appalling and fascinating.

Her gaze jerked to his, and she found him watching her, his lips drawn taut, his eyes pinched.

"Killian," she whispered, a question, a plea.

His gaze never leaving hers, he reached out and traced his index finger across the blood on her arm, then brought it to his mouth and drew it across his lower lip.

On some level, she knew she ought to be repulsed, but the sight of him—the smear of crimson on his lips, the trace of his tongue as he licked it, the look of pleasure on his face as he tasted her—was incredibly sensual.

Yes, she ought to feel disgusted, horrified, afraid, but all she felt was love. Acceptance. Blood held no mysteries or horrors for her. How could it? She had mopped up buckets upon buckets in her time at King's College, not to mention the years she had worked by her father's side.

"Have I shocked you beyond bearing?" he asked.

Wetting her lips, she took a second before she answered, and then she offered the truth.

"Shocked me? Yes. I am shocked, but not so much by what you did, as by the way I feel about it." She paused, and he gave her the moment, gave her time to collect her thoughts. "I am neither horrified nor repulsed, and *that* is the shocking thing. I found it..." She shook her head, trying to understand her own emotions. "Is blood essential to you? For your survival?"

"Yes. But that was not for survival. I did not feed from you, Sarah. That was but a tiny sip. It is a—" he made an absent gesture "—for my kind, it is a form of connection. I come into you and you come into me."

Somehow, she understood that. She *had* felt connected to him, as though for a single glittering instant, they were one.

"You did not feed from me...but you *do* feed?"

"Occasionally." He made a small smile. "Not often. And the bowls of blood the physicians bleed from their patients ought not go to waste."

She felt her lips twitch in an answering smile, and she wondered if she ought to be horrified by that. Her father had always deemed the practice of bloodletting to be both dangerous and barbaric. She could hardly fault Killian for putting the folly of others to a beneficial use.

Suddenly, the magnitude of their discourse overwhelmed her, and she fell back on the sheets to stare at the gilded ceiling.

"That story in the magazine...You are—"

"Nothing like the monster in the story," Killian offered. "But, yes, I am a vampire."

He leaned in as though to kiss her, but held himself inches above her, hovering just beyond reach, his gaze locked on hers.

She understood then. The choice was hers. To deny him or to clasp him to her, press her mouth to his, accept him for all he was.

To accept that he was a vampire.

"Does it cause you pain?" he asked, touching the marks on her skin.

"It...stings," she said.

He bit down on his tongue and licked the wounds he had made on her. To her astonishment the sting disappeared, and the marks with it.

"Oh, let me see!" She surged forward and peeled back his lips and he laughed as she poked at his tongue. "There's no wound."

"I heal from all wounds," he said.

"And you healed my wounds..." Her eyes grew wide. "Killian, imagine! You can cure disease, heal horrific injuries, you can—"

He pressed two fingers to her lips. "I cannot. I can heal only tiny wounds in humans with the application of my blood, and then only if my blood touches the wound from the fount. Anything larger than a prick or a scratch does not respond, and if I bleed myself into a tube or beaker, my blood alters immediately and loses whatever minimal curative power it has."

Sarah thought for a moment, and then nodded. "That makes sense."

Killian's brows rose. "It does?" he asked as he twined his fingers with hers and drew her hand up to kiss her palm.

"Of course. If you are—" she cut him a sidelong glance "—feeding and you are interrupted or have had your fill and wish to save a portion of your meal for later, it makes sense that you could seal a wound so that your prey would not bleed to death and would be available at a different time."

Killian stared at her then he laughed. "You are ever practical."

And Sarah laughed at the wonder in his tone, as though her practicality were some wonderful and desirable treasure.

After a moment she asked, "What we just shared...Was it an act of love for you, the taking of my blood?"

His lashes swept down.

"An act of connection," he said, his voice ragged. "I have lived alone for more years than you can imagine. I dare not let myself love." He looked at her then, his expression so bleak that her heart broke for him. "To love means to lose, Sarah. I cannot. I dare not. It is a path to madness for one such as me." He made a muted groan. "I think that in the years of emptiness, I have forgotten how to love. But I can keep you safe. I can make you happy. Those things I can offer you. And I can offer you truth. I want you."

Tears welled, and she made no effort to stem their flow, but let them trickle from the corners of her eyes and across her temples. She would not hide them from him as he had not hidden the truth from her. He did not love her. Could not love her. But he wanted her.

She lifted her head and pressed her mouth to his. She could taste the faintly metallic hint of her own blood on his lips.

"Sarah—"

"Shh." She pressed her fingers against his lips, then kissed him again. "It matters not, Killian. I have enough love for us both. I *do*. I will share my love with you, and it will be enough. I swear it will be enough."

With a groan, he took her mouth in a hungry kiss. He made love to her once more, languid caresses and leisurely care, no part of her untouched. No part of her unloved.

But beneath his gentle care, she sensed his demons, tightly leashed.

And when they were both sated, the sheets rumpled and mussed, her heart thudding in the aftermath of passion, she stroked his hair and asked, "How long, Killian? How long have you been alone?"

His chest expanded on a deep breath, and she thought he would not answer. There was sadness for her in that, in his refusal to share any part of himself. Then he surprised her, his voice low and deep.

"Five hundred years, Sarah. I have been alone for five hundred years."

The enormity of that slapped her, and she gasped. She could not imagine it, could not think how he had borne it.

"In all that time, you never took a companion, never shared yourself with anyone?"

"Physically, yes. I have taken many lovers. But not a companion. I brought none of them into my home, my haven. I showed only one woman the truth of what I am. She turned from me in disgust and I did not try again, not because I feared another rebuff, but because after a time, I was glad that she had been horrified, glad that she turned from me. I preferred my solitude even as I reviled it." He smiled a little. "Do you understand?"

"I do," she whispered. "Better than you think. I could have found a man to marry me—"

"But it would have cost you everything you are."

"A price I will never be willing to pay," she said.

HOURS LATER, KILLIAN SAT PROPPED ON THE PILLOWS, FEEDING Sarah slices of apple dipped in honey. The sticky liquid clung to her lips, and when he leaned in and kissed her, it clung to his as well. He popped a slice in his mouth, chewed and swallowed, and Sarah watched him with unabashed curiosity.

"You eat," she observed.

He laughed. "Yes."

She laid her palm flat against his chest.

"Your heart beats."

"It does," he agreed, amused. "Despite the stories and mad suppositions, Sarah, I am not undead. My heart beats. And though my body does not require food, I can have the occasional bit if I choose, simply to enjoy the taste."

"Just the occasional bit? That is all you require?"

"I require only blood. And in the beginning I could not tolerate food at all. But over time, I acquired a taste for the occasional morsel, especially sweets." He grinned. "I always had a taste for sweets."

She came up on her knees and studied him. "And sleep? Do you sleep?"

"I sleep when I must, usually a handful of hours each week, always during the daylight hours, for those are the hours when sleep lures me."

"Do you feed every day?"

"I take it as I require, far less often now than in the early years."

She nodded, and dipped her finger in the honey, then smeared it over his lips. Tipping her head, she kissed him, tasting honey, tasting him.

Then his words triggered a thought. "How often did you require it in the early years?" And that question triggered another. "How often do you require it now? How does it work? You said you take it from the bleeding bowls...how long after the patient is bled does the blood remain viable as a source of nourishment for you? Is there a difference when you feed directly from a person? Why blood? Is it the whole of it that you crave or just a single component? And—"

He rested his fingers on her lips, grinning at her. "Ever the physician, my Sarah. So curious."

She laughed. "I *am* curious." She paused. "Alright, answer the first question first. How often did you feed in the early years?"

"At least once each week. More often than that, if possible. It was like a madness, a thirst that could be assuaged no other way. And if I went too long, the madness became a maelstrom."

Sarah tapped her lower lip, his answer sending her thoughts racing along different paths until one snagged her full attention. "The killer at King's College," she mused. "He takes the lives of those who are dying, those who suffer terrible pain. I think he believes it a mercy. But he does it often. Does that mean he is...new? That these are the early years for him?"

Killian blinked, and sat straight. "A newly made vampire. Yes. That makes sense. And he is making an effort to turn his thirst to the good, to find a way to control it."

"Did you control it?" she asked, not quite certain that she wanted to know.

He swung his legs over the side of the bed, planting his bare feet on the carpet, and he turned his face to her over his shoulder, his expression somber.

"Not at first. At first, I was careless and greedy, drinking where I would. I did not murder indiscriminately. I tried to take from those who were already touched by death's hand, or those who ought to be. The murderers. The villains. Those with true evil in their hearts." He raked his hand back through his hair, and took a slow breath, as though deliberating how much to reveal. "I would have you know the truth, Sarah, though it paints me in a less than perfect light. I did not always drain my prey unto death, but I took no pains to ensure that I did not. I simply did not care if they lived or died."

"But the vampire who hunts at King's College does care," she pointed out. "He kills on purpose, and he chooses to drain those who are suffering a horrible death."

"A strange form of morality."

"Killian, I think it is the vampire that follows me. I have seen him in the graveyard, sensed his presence behind me in the alleys. He dogs my steps." She shook her head. "It is the same man, Killian. The man who stalks me is the same as the one who moves like a wraith through the wards, stealing lives." She paused. "But that comes as no surprise to you, does it?"

"It does not. My kind are a territorial lot. We have an ability to sense other blood drinkers who step into a place we consider ours. I sensed him there, outside Mrs. Cowden's house."

She gasped, for though she had suspected it, hearing confirmation was disturbing. "What does he want with me? Why does he follow me?"

Killian reached back and took her hand. "I don't know. I do not think he wishes to drain you. That would have been an easy feat for him and he would have done it long before now were that his intent."

"How very reassuring," she said.

Killian studied her for a moment. "He moves about only in the darkness," he said. "His pattern indicates he is too new to have built up any sort of tolerance of the light."

"That is why you told me I would be safe in the light." And as she thought about it now, she realized it was true. She had never felt the sensation of being watched, being followed, in the daylight. Only in the hours between dusk and dawn. "But *you* can move about in the light."

He smiled at her then. "I can move about in the light, if I am careful and my skin covered, but I am centuries older than he."

Centuries. Her breath locked in her throat. She was not accustomed to that yet. Hundreds of years, alone. She could not imagine it, could not imagine how he had borne it.

"What happens if you are exposed to the light?"

"Much the same as what happens if *you* are exposed for too long. My skin pinkens, then reddens. Blisters form. There is discomfort, then pain. It is not deadly, merely unpleasant. But if I stay in the light for a length of time and do nothing to protect myself, unpleasant turns to deadly. If I stand unprotected in the full light of the sun, I will burn to ash."

"Burn to ash? How long?" She was horrified by the thought of Killian dying in the sunlight.

"How long can I bear the sun? I have experimented over the years and the duration increases exponentially. At present, the longest I have dared is an hour. And then it cost me a month of recovery. But the newly born will burn more quickly." He paused and Sarah sensed that he was about to share something of import. "My maker cast himself into the sunlight and crumbled to ash with moments."

Sarah didn't know what story lay behind those words, but she sensed that it was one that yet caused Killian sadness. She crawled across the bed and wrapped her arms around him, resting her cheek against his back.

"So sunlight can kill him," she said. "What else? A pistol? A knife?"

For a moment, she thought he would not answer, would hold fast the secrets she longed now to know. Then he made a huffing exhalation and said, "There is very little now that can kill him." After a pause, he finished softly, "Another vampire could do the deed."

She shivered, reading his meaning in the things he did not say. "You will kill him, this newly made creature, if he does not agree to cease murdering people."

"Yes and no. He must cease murdering in such a public manner. In truth, I have no argument with his choice of victim."

"I dislike that word," Sarah said with a shiver.

He made a soft sound. "I understand. But I will not lie to you or pretend my kind is other than what we are. Predators."

Sarah nodded. "I know." She paused. "The public manner of the killings...do they concern you because they could reveal the existence of vampires?"

"Even small children suspect that monsters exist. But suspicion is far different than certainty," Killian said. "I cannot leave him free to dart about and kill indiscriminately, leaving *proof* that monsters exist. Therein lies a path to horror, for vampires and humans alike. There are not so many of my kind. I have gone for centuries without encountering another. But stir the terror that lurks inside the human heart and they will begin to see monsters where none exist. They will turn on their neighbors, accuse the innocent, breed fear and mistrust and kill each other. That I cannot allow."

"So you will find him."

"Had he chosen to remove the bodies, or hide the cause of their deaths, that would be a different matter."

"Will you kill him?" Something about that thought disturbed her, though she could not say why.

"You dislike the idea," Killian said, head tipped to one side.

"I don't know why, but I do," Sarah replied. "He frightened me, but never harmed me, and..."

"And?"

"I..." How to explain? "I once thought there was something familiar about him..."

"I have no desire to kill him. And I would like some answers. Who he is. Who made him. Why he claims King's College as his hunting ground." He took her hand and kissed her palm. "Why he follows you."

"Is there danger, Killian? To you?"

"No." She heard the smile in his voice as he replied. "He is newly made, and I... well, I am not."

"I can help," she said, and rushed on as he started to speak, intending, she was certain, to argue. "He will not know that I no longer work at King's College. He will expect me to walk home this evening to Coptic Street, and that is exactly what I will do."

Her heart thudded as she waited for his reply, waited to see if he would see the value of her plan.

A slow smile curved his lips, and he curled his fingers around her nape and drew her close for a hard kiss.

"A brilliant plan. You will walk to Coptic Street—" he cast her a sidelong look through his lashes "—and I will follow in your shadow."

In that moment, she was both pleased that he valued her proposition, that he saw the importance of her participation, and faintly uneasy by the menace she sensed lurking just beneath the surface.

He shifted so his lips moved against her ear as he whispered, "I am what I am, Sarah. No matter how civilized, how controlled the veneer, beneath it all, I am the hunter, the monster, the fiend."

❧ 18 ❧

That night, Sarah walked slowly past the graveyard, searching for some hint of the man who stalked her. The place was silent and still. No shadow, no sound, no movement. He was not there. She was a little surprised, for she had been so certain he would come. But there was still time. He might yet show himself at any point along the route.

He did not. Not that night or the next or the one after that.

Each night, Sarah slept in Killian's bed while he went to King's College and worked with the patients. Her days were spent in his laboratory, a wonderful space that spanned the entire top floor of his home. He had taken her there when she woke the first morning.

"I will not allow your talents to go to waste," he had said. "If there is aught you need that is not here, you have merely to tell me so."

And Sarah had immersed herself in work, free to indulge her interests and aptitude.

On the fourth night, Sarah waited by the doors of King's College until Elinor emerged. "Sarah," her friend cried and rushed to her side to throw her arms around her. "Are you well?" Elinor grasped her by the shoulders and drew back to examine her face. Before Sarah could speak, Elinor gave a muffled laugh. "Oh, you look well. More than well. Dare I say, happy?"

Sarah smiled. "I am well and happy."

Elinor's dimples appeared as she grinned. "Mr. Thayne told me you were well and safe. But I'm glad to see it for myself."

A ball of warmth spread through Sarah's heart. She had not asked Killian to reassure Elinor, yet he had done so. Such a Killian thing to do.

The two women stood talking for a few moments, and with Sarah's assurance that she would call on Elinor one day soon, they separated, Elinor going in one direction, Sarah in the other.

Sarah walked past the graveyard. A thick, damp blanket of fog clung to the tombstones and the surrounding buildings. She braved a glance over her shoulder toward the slaughterhouses. The fog veiled them from sight though she knew they were behind her for the air was stained with the scent of blood and butchered meat.

Beneath her cloak, she carried her cudgel, and her fingers curled tighter about it now. Killian had grinned when he saw it.

"What will you do with that?" he had asked with a low chuckle.

"I shall cosh him on the head if need be."

"Yes, I believe you will." He had caught her to him and kissed her, and held her against his chest, his laughter rumbling through them both.

The sound had poured through her like chocolate, luscious and warm. She made him laugh. She brought him joy. There was such pleasure for her in that.

Now, she walked on, quickening her pace, the chill of the night, or perhaps unease, making her teeth chatter. She resisted the urge to peer about, to search for some sign of Killian. She knew she would see no hint of his presence. He blended seamlessly with the night.

The hunter. She shivered as she recalled his words, uncertain how she felt about that. He would do what he must to keep humans safe from one of his kind, but what did that make him? And what did it make her that she loved him nonetheless?

She turned onto Queen Street and continued toward St. Giles. They had determined that she would take the quickest way to Coptic Street this night, through alleys and courtyards, for that was the darkest route, the most isolated, and their best hope to draw out the man they sought.

Summoning the memory of her previous encounter with him, she recalled that he was tall, draped in a flowing black cloak, his hands gloved, his face shadowed by a low crowned hat. There was little enough to hint at his identity, but for some reason, she felt certain he was familiar. Not Mr. Watts. She had already crossed him off her list. Mr. Simon, perhaps? He was of a height, and there was the fact that, while he attempted to lay suspicion on Killian, he, too, had been present on the ward on the day of each murder.

But that was the conundrum. The *day* of each murder. Even if the deaths occurred during the night, Mr. Simon had been there during the day after the discovery of each body. If he was a newly turned vampire, how then did he manage to stand in the light?

A sound distracted her, and she whirled to see a group of dark, furry bodies nosing at the gutter. Rats. Twitching her skirt aside, she made a soft exhalation then walked on.

Keeping a wary watch on her surroundings, she passed the darkened chandler's shop, and the black windows of the stores that dealt in all manner of birds and small animals. Between the buildings, the alleys and courts darted in all directions, made chilling and menacing by the impenetrable fog.

In the distance, a dog began to howl, a solitary, mournful cry. Shivering, Sarah hesitated and looked about, the hair at her nape prickling and rising. She could hear the sound of her own breathing, harsh and loud.

Drawing her cloak tight about her, she walked on, daring a glance over her shoulder that revealed nothing save darkness and mist. But she sensed him, the man who stalked her. He had come.

And with him came her fear.

The sound of footsteps rang hollowly on the cobbles close behind her.

She froze, attuned to the faintest noise.

The footsteps stopped as she stopped, and when she began her trek once more, the echo of booted heels hitting the stones resumed.

A sharp trill of fear cut her, and she prayed Killian was behind her for she had no wish to confront the man—the *vampire*—on her own. No sooner did the thought coalesce, than the rising tide of her fear dissipated somewhat. Killian *was* watching, blanketed by the night. She had no doubt of that.

Faint sounds carried from the surrounding streets and buildings, raucous laughter, a woman's sobs, a baby's frantic cries. But all she could focus on was the ringing steps of the vampire that followed her, his steps matched to hers, neither falling back nor drawing near.

Just as she and Killian had planned, she turned down the same alley where the man who stalked her had cornered her before. Up ahead, the wooden cart was angled to block the way exactly as it had been the last time she walked this route. The thick vapor swirled around the wheels in ghostly embrace.

She kept her steps even until she reached the wagon, then she spun to face the length of the alley, her back pressed against the rough wood, her pulse hammering a frantic rhythm. She felt isolated here, the fog building a boundary between her and the rest of the world.

Before her, tendrils of mist stirred and parted, and she gasped as a dark shape emerged. Her heart slammed about in her chest like a bird desperate to fly free.

She saw him then, the vampire, there before her, a handful of steps away. His cloak hung about his tall frame and the low crowned hat was pulled down on his brow as it had been when last he hunted her. Panic clawed at her, though she knew Killian was near, knew he would let no harm befall her.

Her breath rushed in and out in short, panting gasps. Her arms trembled as she raised her cudgel, her full attention focused on the man who moved toward her, one step, another, bringing him closer and closer still.

Slowly, he raised his hand toward her. Her heart leapt to her throat.

The sound of cloth flapping in the wind carried to her, and a dark shape plummeted down from above, black cape rising like wings. She gasped and jerked back as Killian landed neatly on the balls of his feet, directly behind her pursuer.

With a hiss of surprise, the man began to turn, but Killian was on him, his lips peeled back in a feral snarl, his arm coming tight around the stranger's throat, holding him fast.

With his hands clasped around Killian's forearm, the man struggled to break his hold. His efforts were in vain. Regardless of how he twisted and clawed, Killian held him.

In the tussle, the stranger's hat knocked free. Shaggy, dark hair tumbled across his brow and his gaze jerked up to lock with Sarah's. Her vision narrowed to a tight black tunnel and she swayed where she stood, overwhelmed.

Shock and disbelief slapped her, and she sagged against the wooden cart as Killian slammed the man against the wall of the alley.

Her cudgel slipped from her hands to clatter against the stones, and she pushed herself upright, stumbled forward.

"Killian, no," she cried. "He is...dear God...he is my *father*."

His forearm still pressed across the other man's throat, Killian turned his head to look at her. His lips were peeled back in a feral snarl, his expression terrifying. But she was not afraid. Not of Killian.

"He is my father," she said again, joy and confusion, anger and shock all mixing together in a bubbling brew.

She almost ran to him, almost threw herself upon him, but Killian shifted so he stood between them and said, "Not yet, Sarah."

She froze in her tracks. Her father bared his teeth as he snarled and clawed at Killian's arm. It was clear that he was not merely trying to free himself, but to cause Killian harm. She recalled then what Killian had told her, how two of his kind could not inhabit the same territory. Her father was newly made. His instincts would surely overpower his logic.

"Killian, he is my father. Please, you cannot..." Cannot kill him.

He cut her a sidelong glance. "I am well aware."

Her father chose that moment to surge at him. Sarah cried out, but Killian had the situation well under control. He was stronger than her father and he had been vampire for far longer.

He shifted his hold, keeping her father pinned with one hand, bringing his other to his lips. He tore open his wrist with his teeth and pressed the wound to her father's lips.

"Drink," he ordered.

Her father struggled for an instant, then with a moan he latched onto Killian's wrist.

"Enough," Killian said after a moment, and her father clutched at him in protest, but Killian was the stronger. He drew his wrist away and after another moment or two, he let go his restraint of her father. "Better?" Killian asked.

Her father made no answer, but he did not surge toward Killian in an attempt to attack, so she supposed it was better.

"It is enough to dampen the blood rage, yes?" Killian asked.

Her father offered a curt nod, then his gaze slid to Sarah, his expression shifting to shock then dismay.

"You are together—" He broke off and stumbled back, looking between Sarah and Killian, shaking his head from side to side as though trying to clear a noise from his ears. "You are *with* my daughter, yet you are like me? A vampire?" His tone was edged with horror.

"I am vampire," Killian confirmed.

For a moment, the three of them stood in an awkward, motionless tableau then her father turned to her and held his hand out in supplication. "Sarah—"

She was dizzy under the onslaught of emotion that buffeted her. A thousand words tumbled to her lips, but she could manage only one.

"Why?" she cried, her gaze locked on her father, her nerves frayed and twisted in a Gordian knot. "Why follow me? Frighten me? Never reveal yourself to me?

"Sarah," he said, his voice rough, the single word imbued with pain and distress and love. Then he pressed his lips tight and said nothing more.

She advanced on him, her shock and joy at finding him alive melding with feeling of both anger and betrayal. "Why?" she demanded. "Why did you let me believe you were dead? Drowned? I mourned you. I cried a river of tears. My heart was broken."

"No, I—" He brought his hands up before him, a gesture of despair.

"How could you—" She broke off and simply shook her head, too confused, too overcome by hurt and betrayal to formulate the slurry of her thoughts into any semblance of coherent speech.

Again, she advanced, but Killian stopped her with a gesture. "He is vampire," he said, and his meaning struck her. Her father was a vampire. She was human. Her blood was human, a siren's song to one such as he.

Horror clawed at her and she fell back a step.

"No!" her father said. "I would never—"

"You cannot know that," Killian said, his voice cold. He withdrew something from his cloak, and as he held it out, an offering to her father, Sarah saw that it was a flask. "Drink," he ordered.

Her father looked back and forth between the two, then he accepted the flask from Killian and took a tentative sip. His eyes widened and he drank the whole of it down in greedy gulps.

Killian strode to Sarah's side as he offered a command, his tone ice and steel. "Do not move from that spot, Mr. Lowell. Certainly, do *not* force me to stop you." He pulled Sarah against him, wrapping her in the haven of his embrace.

She could not say how long they stood thus. Perhaps only seconds, perhaps far longer. At length, she felt her control return. Drawing a shaky breath, she stepped free of the shelter of Killian's wonderfully safe embrace, her gaze lifting to meet her father's tormented stare.

"I thought you were an opium addict. I thought that under the influence of that foul drug you fell in the Thames and drowned." She paused. "You *let* me think that."

"I did. And I am sorry." Her father held his hand out to her, tears glittering on his lashes. Even in the paltry light, she could see his pallor and the deep black circles beneath his eyes. He had suffered, and it hurt her to know it. "I was never an opium addict, Sarah. I wanted you to think it because it was the only way to shield you. The symptoms you saw were...it was the *hunger.* I cannot explain it. It is like nothing I have ever experienced. It only grew stronger, a gnawing pain that ripped me to bits until I dared not be near you, dared not trust myself. My God, you have no idea what I have become. I *did* want to die. I tried. Flung myself in the Thames. Only...I came to understand that this thing I have become will not die." He drew a great shuddering breath. "My God, I have missed you so."

"Do not lie to yourself or to her," Killian said, his voice low. "You knew there was a way to die."

Her father drew a breath, then blew it out. "Alright. Yes. I knew I could stand in the sun. It didn't take long to find that out. But I—"

"Didn't want to die," Killian finished for him.

"I didn't want to die," her father agreed.

"Papa," Sarah said past the lump in her throat, her hand reaching for him.

He lurched forward. Moving so fast he was little more than a blur, Killian insinuated himself between them, using his body as a shield.

"Do you trust yourself, Mr. Lowell?" he asked, darkly soft.

"She is my daughter," her father said.

"She is *mine*," Killian said in a tone she had never before heard from him. That single word revealed the beast inside him, the primitive creature driven by instinct, driven to claim and to hold what he claimed. He looked down at her then. "She is my light, my joy, my heartbeat. I will let nothing harm her."

"I will not harm her. I have sat by her bed as she slept. I have followed her through this vile place—" her father gestured at their surroundings "—to keep her safe."

"You sat by my bed?" *Sleep now, Sarah. Dream sweet dreams.* "You did. I remember."

Overwhelmed, Sarah looked back and forth between the two. Her lover was a vampire, and her father had returned from the dead.

"How were you turned to a vampire, Papa?" she asked. "How did you become what you are?"

"The patient from France. You remember? The friend that Mr. Montmarche begged me to see." His mouth twisted and his tone turned to a sneer. "My kindness was repaid by betrayal. He was a vampire, burned by the sun. His skin was blackened and falling away, and he was desperate for blood. He drained me nearly unto death."

Sarah shuddered at his words, for the images they conjured were ghastly. She recalled the dead patients at King's College, their wrists torn open, bloodless.

"Papa," she said, pouring her sadness and empathy into that single word.

With a sigh, her father reached out for her. Beside her Killian tensed, ready to leap to her protection.

To protect her from her father.

She edged around Killian, weaving her fingers through his, then reached out with her free hand to her father. "You cannot know," she whispered to Killian. "I thought him dead, and here he is. Alive." She swallowed against the lump that clogged her throat. "I thought I would never see him again. I never even had a body to bury." She paused. "I thought I was alone."

Laying his hand on her back, Killian said nothing, but she could feel the tension that pulsed beneath the surface, sense the beast he had warned her lurked beneath the thin veneer. He did not trust her father, and she understood that, understood his need to hold her safe.

Warily, her father approached and took her hand. Tears traced along her cheeks. She held the hands of both men.

"You say he drained you nearly unto death, but how is it that you became what he was?" she asked her father.

"Montmarche's friend—" her father made a dull laugh "—you know, I never did learn his name. Well, he gave me the choice. To die, or to take his blood and live. I chose life. But I did not understand. Not until I woke with the thirst." He exhaled sharply through his nostrils. "He was long gone by then, and I was left with the thirst and a thousand questions."

Killian made a small sound of disgust. "The newly made making more newly made. A dangerous folly."

"Sarah, my darling, I would not have left you alone had I a choice," her father said. "But it was better for me to die, to remove myself from your life. I have watched you from the shadows. Guarded you as best I could. I dared not be near you, for I was afraid both of what I might do to you, and of what you might think of the aberration I have become. But...you already know. You—" His gaze shot to Killian.

"Mr. Lowell," Killian interjected. "You have been killing patients at King's College."

With a gasp, Sarah shook her head, reminding herself exactly why they had lured him to this place. Because of the murders. *Murders.* And Killian meant to end the string of deaths by terminating the killer.

"What? King's College?" Her father scrubbed his palms over his face. Dropping his hands, he glanced first at Sarah, then Killian. He seemed to sink into himself as he made a gesture of futility. "Yes. I saw no other course, no way to slake the hunger. I took only those who were suffering. Only those who would die regardless. You know, I can sense that now. I can feel death clinging to every breath. I know who will not survive, no matter what medical machinations are offered."

Sarah glanced at Killian. That was how he knew which patients would not benefit from any intervention. He, too, could sense death.

"So you chose with care." Killian's lips turned in a faint smile, and his tone was one of understanding. "I admire both your restraint and your compassion. It is common for the newly turned to feed in a mad frenzy without thought or care. That you held yourself from that is admirable."

Something in his tone made Sarah's breath catch. Something dark.

Admirable or not, he would kill her father.

She could not let him. But, oh God, her father was himself a murderer.

Her gaze jerked to Killian's, and she found him studying her, his eyes flat, his expression ruthlessly neutral. There was a sinister side to what he was. He had warned her of that.

"Killian," she whispered, even as her father said, "Sarah—"

Killian's gray eyes gleamed in the darkness, holding her trapped, breathless. He had told her this. He had told her of the murderers and thieves that he had fed from. Was her father to be his next victim?

"No, love. That is not the way of it," Killian said with a shake of his head.

Love. She drew a sharp breath, stunned by the term. Killian would not use it lightly.

"For five centuries I have been alone." He cast a sidelong glance at her father. "And now I go from being completely alone, to having a complete family, including a father-in-law who is a fledgling I must needs tutor." He made a wry smile. "There is a certain dark irony in that."

Her thoughts whirling, Sarah could only gape at him, trying to understand his meaning.

Killian inclined his head to her father, and said, "If you would afford us a moment of privacy, sir?"

Without waiting for a reply, he took her hand and drew her off into the shadows.

"You called him your father-in-law," Sarah said.

"I did. I'll marry you if you'll have me."

Sarah lifted her brows and pressed her lips together. "Was that meant to be a proposal?"

Killian laughed softly. "The first I've ever made to any woman. And the last." His gaze grew somber, and the teasing glint disappeared. "Do not answer me right away, love, only listen to what I offer. I want to turn you."

"Turn me?" Even as she echoed the words, his meaning became clear. He wanted her to be as he was. "Killian—"

"Please—" he pressed his fingers to her lips "—hear me out." He brought her hand to his lips and kissed her palm. "You asked me if I loved you. I knew I wanted you. I knew I respected you. I knew I treasured you. I did not believe I loved you because I did not believe myself capable of love."

She swallowed, staring up at him, her heart thudding a painful rhythm.

"But in this alley when faced with the need to terminate the interloper, I could not because of the pain it would cause you. When faced with the instinct to stop the creature that could expose us all, I could not because of the pain it would cause you. When I realized that he was your father, the joy that swelled inside me on your behalf was brighter than a sunrise. What I feel for you is deeper than instinct, stronger than my hunger, greater than any need I have ever known. If it would benefit you in some way, I would walk into the sun. So it appears that the monster is capable of love after all."

"Killian," she whispered, choking on her tears. He leaned in and kissed them where they traced down her cheek.

"I want to share eternity with you," he said. "To show you the world. To never see you grow a day older than you are now. To watch civilizations evolve and change until there are women who are physicians and surgeons and you are one of them." His expression grew solemn. "But there is a price. Both your father and I were turned without knowing the full extent of what we would become. If you choose this, love, if you choose me, I need you to make that choice with full understanding.

"So say nothing yet, my love. Make no hasty decision." He pulled her against him, and brushed his lips across hers. "Stay with me, Sarah. Be my light, my love. And when you are ready, only then give me your answer."

Her heart swelled and she could only offer a mute nod. It was too much, too much. Killian loved her. He loved her and he wanted her for exactly who she was. And he offered her the world.

She rose up on her toes and pressed her mouth to his, then whispered, "I love you," against his lips.

EPILOGUE

One year later

SARAH SNUGGLED CLOSE AGAINST KILLIAN'S SIDE, LANGUID AND replete in the aftermath of their lovemaking. Reaching up, she dragged her fingers through the thick golden silk of his hair, loving the feel of it.

Loving him.

A year they had been together, and each day was a gift, a treasure. They had married in a church in a small ceremony attended by her father and Mrs. Cowden and Elinor. Killian had opened a small surgery in St. Giles and Sarah worked there alongside him, offering care to women the world had forgotten. Elinor had left King's College for a position at the surgery.

In that year, Killian had told her much of what it meant to be a vampire. The joys, the beauty, the freedom. The burden, the loneliness, the temptation.

Nothing ever came without a price.

But he had never again voiced the offer to make her what he was, and she had never asked.

Until now.

Rolling so she lay atop him, she stared into his eyes, his beautiful pewter and ice eyes, then she leaned down and pressed her mouth to his.

"It is time, Killian." She drew her long hair to the side, baring the column of her throat. "It is time, my love. I want forever, with you."

He smiled, and dragged his fingers along her pulse where it throbbed beneath the fragile skin of her throat.

"You are certain?"

"I am. I would know the cool and wonderful beauty of the moonlight, the sweet music of the night," she whispered, offering back to him the words he had shared so long ago. "You are no longer alone. I would be with you always, Killian. Always and forever."

The End

Join Eve's Reader Group for the latest info about contests, new releases and more! www.EveSilver.net

If you enjoyed Killian's and Sarah's story,
please leave an online review
to help other readers decide on the book.
Word of mouth is an author's best friend.

Love my gothics? Keep reading for a sneak peek of KISS ME GOODBYE, the first book in my upcoming Contemporary Gothic series!

KISS ME GOODBYE SNEAK PEEK

PROLOGUE
THE SHAPE OF A HEART

I forgot to kiss her goodbye.

Rain pelts my yellow slicker as I hesitate halfway up the steps on the first day of third grade at my new school. Around me, other kids run hand in hand with their mothers or fathers, heading for the front door, trying to escape the downpour. Some of them wear yellow slickers and rubber rain boots just like mine. Some of them are sheltered by the umbrellas their parents hold above their heads.

There's no one to shelter me, to hold my hand. I'm alone, and I forgot to kiss her goodbye.

Should I go forward? Back?

I stand frozen.

Mommy's battered gray car with the rusted rear door and the dented bumper is still parked in front of the school. Through the misted window I see the pale smudge of her face. She's watching me, waiting to see me safely inside.

I run down the stairs toward the car, hoping she'll push the door open, step out, come to me. Foolish hope. I know by now that wishes don't come true.

When I reach the car I press the tip of my finger to the window and draw the shape of a heart, raindrops clinging to my lashes and running down my cheeks. Then I press my lips to the wet glass and kiss her goodbye. She smiles with her mouth but not with her eyes. For her, even the car is too open a space. I smile back because I made her smile, if only a little.

Then I turn and run up the stairs as the morning bell chimes, loving her and hating her and telling myself it isn't her fault.

~

CHAPTER ONE

PROMISE

THE ANCIENT PICKUP BARRELS ALONG THE NARROW HIGHWAY THAT clings to the edge of a cliff. On my right, the earth juts skyward, a wall of gray and brown and green. On my left, a single lane separates me from the white churn of the ocean that crashes against the rocks below.

Wind gusts off the water, making the pickup shiver and shake. The seatbelt isn't working and there's no grab handle so I curl my fingers into the worn seat and hold on. As if that will save me if we go over the edge. The driver—Rick, according to how he introduced himself when he picked me up at the airport in San Francisco; Richard Parsons, according to the letter my aunt sent—slaps his breast pocket, hauls out a cigarette one-handed, tucks it between his lips and pushes in the lighter to heat it up. He takes a deep lungful of smoke and blows it out, adding new cigarette stink to the old cigarette stink that mixes with the scents of sweat and mildew and sickly sweet rot coming off the fast food wrappers on the floor.

Rain pounds the windshield, the wipers smearing hazy arcs.

It's the rain that makes me remember that day. I wonder if I made the wrong choice, if Mom would have stepped out of the car had I not run back to her, if she would have lived a different life if I'd only waited on those stairs, waited for her to come to me. But in my heart of hearts, I know I could have stood there for hours, even days, and she would have stayed trapped in her cocoon, tears streaming down her cheeks, eyes darting side to side, seeing things only she could see.

She must have driven home after she left me at school. She never drove again. I walked home alone that day using my memory of the landmarks she'd pointed out and the map she'd sketched on the torn corner of a piece of pink construction paper. She was waiting for me just inside the door to our building and she grabbed me and pulled me close as soon as I crossed the threshold. I walked alone to school and back the next day and every day after. The car sat untouched for six months and then Mom called someone and a tow truck came and hooked it up and that was the end of that. Mom said it was a good thing, a smart thing, because owning a car when you lived hand to mouth was just a mess of crazy.

Staring straight ahead at the yellow dividing line that unfurls like a ribbon, I swallow against the lump in my throat. It moves down a few inches to sit behind my breastbone, leaden.

Might-have-beens don't matter, Luce. Don't look back, baby. Never look back. Just forward, always forward. Mom wasn't much one for nostalgia. No photo albums. No rogue's gallery of baby pictures on the wall. We never ordered the class picture I suffered through each year. She never even showed me a picture of my dad, Joss Warner, though I figure I must look like him since Mom was blond, blue-eyed, and china doll pretty, and I'm brown-haired with hazel eyes.

Choices. Did I make the wrong one coming here?

Beside me, Rick hacks up a lung, then takes a final drag of his cigarette and stubs it out in the overflowing ashtray.

"You're a real chatterbox, huh?" he says as he hunches forward against the wheel and peers through the windshield, his stained ball cap shadowing his craggy face. I don't like him, don't like the way he looked at me when he found me at the airport or the sneer in his voice when he said my aunt's name. *Pat,* he'd said, like he was horking up a loogie. But he's my ride north and I have no other way to get where

I'm going. If I'd had another option, I'd have taken it. But I didn't, and I don't, and it's a waste of effort to wish otherwise.

The truck skids as we round another curve, number one million and six of the curves we've rounded on this endless drive. I slap my hand against the window for balance and say, "We could slow down."

Rick glances at me then back at the road. "No need." He thumps a closed fist against the dash. "She's been getting me where I need to be for almost twenty years."

I grew up knowing not to walk down Mermaid Avenue at night, to never trust that the N, Q or R would be on time, to fade into the background when the situation called for it, and to speak up for myself when there wasn't anyone else to speak up for me. So I speak up now, making my voice calm even though my heart trip-hammers as I say, "I'd like you to slow down. I'd like to get there alive."

Rick's mouth twists and he turns his head toward me, this man I don't know, don't need to know in order to read his expression: anger, and something else, something darker.

He points his right index finger at me, close to my face. "You—"

The wind gusts, catching us on a rare stretch of straight road. The pickup swerves to the right, almost slamming up against the wall of earth that spikes toward the sky. The truck goes one way and I go the other, digging in my fingers to keep myself from sliding all the way across the bench seat and slamming into Rick. He swears and jerks the wheel to the left, sending the truck in the opposite direction, across the yellow line, closer to the flimsy rail that's all that holds us back from the jagged rocks and crashing surf.

The back end fishtails, the truck gliding over wet asphalt like skates on ice. With a snarl, he jerks the wheel to the right and we're back in our lane, speeding along the deserted, rain-slick road.

My breath comes in short gasps.

The needle of the speedometer eases down a couple of notches.

I don't say anything. He doesn't say anything. We drive.

I shiver and I know he sees it. I don't want him to think it's from fear because people like him feed on that.

"There's a draft," I say, reaching up to poke at the faulty seal between the doorframe and the window that's been leaking icy drops since the rain began. Water pools on my fingertip, slides down across my palm, along my wrist, my forearm, my elbow, before dripping off onto my denim-clad thigh.

This morning I'd dressed for what I thought was late June California weather: black t-shirt, denim cut-offs that stop mid-thigh, my purple plaid Converse, my wavy hair in a ponytail, the ever present curly-frizzy bits escaping at the sides. Then I'd locked the apartment door for the very last time. It was empty. I'd sold everything I could, and what didn't find a buyer, I'd donated or dragged to the Dumpster. Everything I own is smooshed into the massive, camping-sized backpack I'd discovered in a second-hand store. It sits now between my feet, the top grazing my knees.

I stare out the window at the rain, not really seeing anything.

I'd left Brooklyn thirteen hours ago.

A bus ride and plane ride and truck ride ago.

A lifetime ago.

I shiver again, and this time it really is from the cold. It didn't take long after we left San Francisco behind for me to figure out that I don't know shit about Northern California weather. I unzip the pack, pull out my black hoodie, and shrug it on.

In the pocket is the letter my aunt sent, folded in half and in half again. I'd read it twice on the plane, adding to the dozen or so times I'd read it in the week since it arrived. Each subsequent read yielded no more information than the first.

A letter. Not an email. Not a phone call.

Aunt Patience wrote me a letter in response to the letter I sent her because the only contact info I had was a yellowed slip of paper with a hand-written mailing address. I found it in the drawer of Mom's bedside table. I tried to get a phone number for my aunt so I could call, but either my search engine skills failed me, or my aunt doesn't have a landline. I pretty much wrote: *your sister is dead.* She pretty much wrote back in her cramped, wobbly, back-slanted cursive: *I didn't know she was sick. Here is a plane ticket to San Francisco, though I no longer live there. I am in Carnage Bay now. Your uncle poses no objection to you coming. A man, Richard Parsons, will fetch you from the airport.*

The abundance of warmth and welcome in that brief paragraph left me all soft and fuzzy inside. The first time I read her reply, I wondered why my aunt didn't call me or email, why she wouldn't meet me at the airport herself. I wondered briefly if Richard Parsons was my uncle, but my aunt's wording—*a man, Richard Parsons*—made me think not. There was no time to write her back to ask the questions churning in my thoughts and then wait for her to mail her reply. Not if I wanted to make that flight. Any answers I'm going to get will have to wait until I see her in person.

I almost decided not to come. I could have taken the $738.00 I have to my name and gone anywhere.

I could have just disappeared with no one the wiser, no one to care.

But I made a promise, and I keep my promises, even when they make no sense.

"I need to know you'll be safe," Mom said when she told me to go find her sister. "You'll be happy with Patience. You were always happy to see her. Remember?"

I haven't seen Aunt Pat in eight years, maybe more. I have fuzzy memories of a young, pretty blond woman. Girl, actually. At the time, she must have been just a little older than I am now. I remember big blue eyes like Mom's, but Aunt Pat's turned up a little at the corners, especially when she laughed. She laughed a lot. Mom laughed with her, which was rare enough both before and after Aunt Pat's visits that the image stands clear and bold in my thoughts.

I remember that my aunt visited every few weeks for a while, in the time before Mom stopped going outside altogether. The fading strains of the music at the carousel in Central Park dance at the edges of my memories, Aunt Pat riding the horse next to mine, Mom standing on the side, expression pinched and nervous, arms crossed and pressed tight to her midsection.

I remember that when Aunt Pat told me she was going away, that she wouldn't see me but that she'd write to me, I cried into my pillow.

After she left, she kept her word, writing us long, colorful letters, happy stories of travel and excitement with a man she called My Prince. Houston, Las Vegas, Reno, San Francisco. Mom read those letters aloud to me like bedtime stories. After a couple of years they came less and less often, then not at all. I don't know if Mom and Aunt

Pat had a falling out or if distance drifted between them. It's a long way from Brooklyn to California.

Of course, it wasn't the distance that kept Mom from taking me for a visit...from taking me anywhere...ever.

Maybe my aunt will be able to explain the why of that. Just days before she died, Mom stared hard at me and said, "Pat has answers."

"To what questions?" I asked.

"Questions and secrets and things best left buried." Mom closed her eyes, the lids thin and papery. I drew the sheet higher. She grabbed my wrist with surprising strength and whispered, "Think carefully before you dig them up." Her lids flipped open and she turned her head, her eyes locking on mine. "Promise you'll go to her. *Promise.*"

She clutched at my hand, her fingers more bone than flesh, blue veins stark against gray-white skin. By then I'd stopped pretending that Mom was going to get better. Still, she refused to go to the hospital, refused to leave the apartment, sending the EMTs away when they came in response to my call.

She was more afraid of going outside than she was of dying.

"You used to call her Patty Cake. Do you remember?"

Her words made my chest tighten. Mom didn't do nostalgia. I nodded even though I didn't remember calling my aunt that and Mom nodded back, happy with my little white lie.

"You'll be happy with her. With family. And she'll tell you..."

She closed her eyes and I thought she'd fallen asleep. Then her lips —blue and chapped—moved and I leaned over to catch her words. "You didn't promise to find her. I need you to promise, Lucian."

So I promised.

Within weeks, orphaned, alone, my mother's whispery demand haunting me, I used the one way ticket my aunt sent, got on a plane, and ended up here.

"Lucian," Rick says, jarring me from my thoughts. "That's a boy's name, ain't it? You're not a boy dressed as a girl, are you?"

I realize that I haven't paid attention to him or the rain or the road, lost in my own thoughts for who knows how many miles. The highway has veered inland, away from the ocean. We're surrounded by trees now, and ahead of me where the road heads north...more trees, thick-trunked and tall.

Rick watches me, waiting for an answer. I almost ask him if I look like a boy, but I recall the feel of his eyes on me at the airport, raking me and stopping in places that creeped me out, so instead I say, "Lucian means light."

I don't tell him it was my brother's name. Lucian Lafayette Warner. The brother I never met. The one who died three years before I was born without ever taking his first breath. And it was my sister's name. The sister I never met. The one who died two years before I was born, her tiny body just shy of two pounds. At least, that's the way Mom told it. She said I was lucky number three. The one who lived. She named me Lucian just like she named them Lucian. Because Mom was bat-shit crazy.

"I prefer Luce," I say.

"Well, Lucian"—Rick bares his teeth—"I need gas and I need to take a shit. You might want to use the facilities yourself. Or you can wait till we get you to your aunt. We're almost there now."

He pulls off the road and circles around to the side of a squat brown building with a white sign on top that proclaims: *Easy Mart.* The rain's let up, but concrete clouds edged in charcoal hang heavy in the sky, promising that there's more to come.

~

CHAPTER TWO

Take A Picture

ONCE THE TRUCK IS PARKED, I PUSH OPEN THE DOOR, GLAD FOR THE chance to stretch my legs. I pause, staring at my backpack, a wave of uncertainty crashing through me. Everything I own is in that pack. What if Rick drives away? What if he leaves me stranded? I don't even have a phone number for my aunt. All I have—

All I have is her letter and on it, her address. I'll find my way there and if Rick takes off with my backpack, my aunt can help me figure out a way to get it back. I repeat that to myself until my nerves settle.

Panic and fear swallowed my mother's life whole. I won't let them do the same to mine. I have goals, dreams, hopes, and I *will* see them come true. I'll find a job and keep saving. I'll go to college. I'll build myself a life that makes me happy, brick by brick, stone by stone.

I slide my wallet out of the pack, shove it into my pocket, then slam the door shut and lift my head to find Rick standing by the truck, his sneer telling me that he's guessed the direction of my thoughts. He drags the back of his hand across his nose then wipes it on his jeans. Turning my back on him, I walk around the corner of the building.

The door to the Easy Mart creaks as I push it open. There's no one at the cash, but I can hear sounds of movement through the open door behind the counter and I figure the cashier is back there. The smell of coffee teases me. I walk over to the pot, thinking a precious dollar might be well spent on something to warm me from the inside out. I squash that thought like a bug. A dollar is a dollar. I need to save each one. The only person contributing to my college fund is me.

I close my eyes and take a deep breath through my nose, enjoying the aroma. Then I turn and walk back outside to stand beside the bench under the overhang and wait for Rick. The gas pumps are off to my left and he hasn't pulled up to them yet. I figure he's still taking care of the other task he mentioned with such delicate manners.

A couple of minutes later, the door of the Easy Mart creaks again as it opens. I glance over to see a man step out, his face weathered and lined, his body greyhound thin. In his hand is a paper cup with steam coming off the top. He holds it out toward me. "You look like you could use this." When I make no move to accept his offering, he adds, "No charge."

"I can pay." The second the words are out I want to haul them back. If I'd wanted to waste a dollar on coffee, I would have.

One side of his mouth crooks up. "Didn't mean to ruffle your feathers, girl. It's just a cup of coffee. I put in a couple packets of sugar and some cream. You look like the sugar and cream type."

Actually, I like my coffee hot and strong and black. One out of three is better than none, so I take the cup as is. "Thank you."

"Take a load off." He juts his chin toward the bench.

"I've been sitting most of the day. I'd rather stand."

"I've been standing most of the day. I'd rather sit." He settles himself at the opposite end of the bench, as far from me as he can get. I figure that's for my comfort, not his. But you never can tell. People have all sorts of weird quirks. "You hitchhiking?" he asks, glancing first at the empty gas pumps then the empty parking lot.

I blow across the surface of the coffee, watching the steam curl up. "My ride's parked around the side. He's...occupied," I say, for lack of a better description.

"You passing through or staying for a stretch?"

I cut him a sidelong glance.

He holds his hands up, palms forward. "Don't need to tell me if you don't want. It's just that I know pretty much everyone around here. Only two other gas stations in Carnage Bay, and one more outside town limits to the north. At some point pretty much everyone shows up here for a fill. So if you're visiting, I'd like to put your face to a name and link that name to one I already know." He waggles his brows and says with unabashed glee, "I'm a busybody."

Carnage Bay. Rick said we were almost there, but I hadn't quite trusted him. "A busybody, huh?" I lift my coffee as if offering a toast. "I'd never have guessed."

Easy Mart laughs. "So?" he prods. "Staying or going?"

I almost don't answer because sharing information with strangers has never been a personal goal. Then I remember my aunt lives here. I live here now. Offending the locals on day one might not be my best plan. Besides, I'll be needing a job and the Easy Mart might have an opening.

"I'm here to stay with my aunt," I say.

"For how long?"

I shrug.

"Tell me your aunt's name"—Easy Mart's whole face creases into a smile—"and I'll tell you some gossip." He winks.

The corners of my mouth twitch. His good humor is kind of infectious and I can use something to smile about.

Just then, Rick's truck eases into view. He parks in front of the pump and ambles over to open the gas cap.

Easy Mart's eyes follow him, and he isn't smiling any more. He pushes to his feet and when he looks at me again, his brows are drawn together, carving deep grooves above the bridge of his nose. "Is that your ride?"

I swallow, the coffee turning bitter and a little salty on my tongue. "Yes."

"Your aunt's name?" he asks, his expression neutral, his tone firm. He isn't joking any more. And suddenly I want to tell him because I want to hear what he has to say about her. Rick hasn't exactly been a chatty font of information on our drive north.

"Patience Warner." Only as I say her name does it hit me: Mom's married name was Warner. It's my last name. So how can her little sister's name be Warner? Yet that's the name that was on the yellowed scrap of paper I found in the nightstand, the name I addressed the letter to. I didn't notice the oddity at the time. Guess I was too busy burying my mother and selling everything we owned. Anyway, I doubt it's a riddle Easy Mart can answer, but maybe he can answer some other questions. I try for a smile, but my face feels stiff. "I'll take the gossip you promised now."

Easy Mart shakes his head, and his eyes slide from mine. "I don't want to make trouble."

"Wait," I say as he steps away. He stops, his back to me, his shoulders bunched and raised. "What sort of trouble?"

He looks back at me over his shoulder and from the tense set of his lips and the clench of his jaw, I can see he's warring with speaking or staying silent. Silent wins. He reaches for the door handle.

"Wait," I say again. "Please."

"Your aunt's name's Patience Davey now, not Warner. You have a care around Mr. Davey." I hear the growl of a motor and Easy Mart's attention jerks to a point behind me, his expression darkening even more. But I don't turn to see what has him frowning. I feel like this guy has something important to share and if I look away even for a second, he'll decide not to tell me anything. After a long pause he grunts. "You take care around anyone with the Davey name."

He pushes open the door. I think he's had his say, but then he turns back toward me without crossing the threshold and the spring pulls the door shut with a snap. He stares at me, his lips drawn in a thin, pale line. Then he rubs the lower half of his face, his fingers sliding down off his jaw. "Why don't you wait here, Patience Davey's niece? Let Rick Parsons be on his way and you stay right here. There's a boy comes by to take the evening shift at seven. I'll take you home to my wife. Feed you some dinner. Then take you back the way you came. Send you back home." He nods, and I can see he's liking this plan more and more as he formulates it. "Yes, I'll send you home. You'll be happy I did."

Can't say I'm not tempted. Head back to Brooklyn, to the known and familiar. I have some good friends there. Abby. Nagar. Daph. I could find a shitty little room somewhere. Work a shitty little job. Figure out what it is I want to study and apply for school. A big part of me wishes I could grab hold of Easy Mart's offer with both hands and just go home.

But home is gone, the apartment already rented to someone else, everything that made it home buried, sold or tossed.

Besides, I promised Mom I'd find Aunt Pat, and that's exactly what I intend to do.

"My aunt's the only home I have now," I say, uncharacteristically open with this man whose name I don't know, my tongue feeling thick and sluggish in my mouth. "She's expecting me."

Easy Mart's shoulders move—up, down—as he takes a heavy breath. "Well..." He shoots a last look toward the gas pumps and Rick Parsons, and then yanks the door open once more. "That's a shame. A damn shame."

This time the door snaps shut only after he's gone inside and I'm left alone under the overhang.

I slump down on the bench and sip at the coffee; it doesn't taste so great between the cream and sugar and the sour edge of Easy Mart's weird warnings. I curl my fingers around the cup, absorbing what little heat I can as I study the motorcycle parked in front of the second pump, the kind of bike that looks like it's built for speed. A spray of mud from the wet road feathers the black paint. The rider climbs off, his face obscured by a black helmet. His black t-shirt is plastered against his back and chest, his jeans dark from the rain.

Rick says something to him as he puts the nozzle in the tank. I'm too far away to hear what it is, but the rider pulls off his helmet, sets it on the seat of his bike, and digs into his pocket, struggling a bit with the wet denim. He passes something to Rick, who hands back a folded bill. It's an exchange I've seen a hundred times before, on street corners or in shadowed nooks.

The rider replaces the nozzle and saunters to the door, passing close enough that I can make out the details of the tattoo on his left forearm: a dark red stylized skull in a field of bright flowers. The ink runs all the way from his wrist, past his elbow, up his arm until it disappears under the short sleeve of his t-shirt. It's beautiful.

"Take a picture." The words aren't exactly friendly, but there's a smile in his voice that tempers them.

My gaze jerks up, but he's through the door and all I see is shaggy dark hair, wide shoulders, and a hand reaching back to pull a wallet from a back pocket.

When he comes out a couple of minutes later, I catch a glimpse of his scowl before he turns away. Guess Easy Mart guy wasn't too friendly to any friend of Rick's.

He rides slowly past me, heading for the road. His visor's down and I can't see his eyes, but I can feel him watching me.

"New girl on display. Take a picture." I'm pretty sure he doesn't hear me over the sound of his engine, somewhere between a growl and a visceral rumble. Besides, there isn't much heat to my words; he already stole my line.

I toss the still almost full coffee cup in the trash and head for Rick's truck, our paths crossing as he heads inside to pay for his gas. He changes direction so he's within inches of me as we pass. I shift at the waist to avoid brushing shoulders with him.

He stops and leers at me. "Makes the rounds, that boy does," he says.

I shrug and keep walking.

When I get to the truck I find that Rick locked the doors, so I rest my forearms on the roof and watch until the lights on the back of the motorcycle disappear around a curve in the road.

oOo

The highway carries us back toward the ocean. *Welcome to Carnage* —I read the sign as we pass. It actually says, *Welcome to Carnage Bay,* but the first three words are painted dark blue and the word 'bay' is this thin script done in pale blue. Hard to see, unless you're really looking.

"Who named this place?"

Rick squints at me. "Why?"

"Carnage Bay? Carnage means killing or murder or something. Who'd give a place like this"—I gesture out the window at the pretty little houses with their white picket fences. Seriously. White picket fences. Even under the heavy press of the bleak sky, this place is too pretty to be real—"a name like that?"

"Dunno. Maybe someone with a sense of humor." Rick smirks around the cigarette dangling out of the corner of his mouth. "Kind of like someone who'd give their girl a boy's name."

I shoot him a look that conveys my every justifiably denigrating thought, but he's watching the road instead of me. "You don't know the history of the name of your town?"

"Not my town," he says. "I've only been living here for just under a year. Came here around the same time your uncle and aunt did."

My aunt has been here a year? That doesn't make sense. The paper I found in Mom's drawer, the one with Aunt Pat's address, was yellowed with age. "But—" I cut myself off. Whatever questions I have will hold until I see my aunt. I don't exactly think of Rick as a reliable source of information.

"But what?" He watches me, eyes narrowed.

"Forget it." I turn away from his too sharp gaze and stare out the window.

We pass a red building with a sign that proclaims: Town Hall. Then we pass a newer building with orange brick, green trim, gray roof, and glass block windows—the Carnage Bay Police Station.

"Carnage is big enough to warrant a police department of its own?" I feel sure the population was on the sign, but I didn't notice it as we passed.

Rick grunts. "Got ourselves one Chief, and maybe a dozen offi-cers." He laughs, a phlegmy sound that makes me inch closer to the door. "You see a car with a light on top coming, you walk the other way, Lucian. Your uncle don't care much for cops."

Reassuring.

I turn my head and watch the town pass. A snort escapes me. I can't help it. Between the trees, the picket fences, and the Town Hall, I feel like I've landed in a foreign country.

Up ahead is a low white building with a packed parking lot. The sign above it reads: *Grocery. Produce. Liquor. Beer. Wine. Pizza. Deli. Hot food.* An all-in-one stop shop.

There's a black motorcycle parked out front.

A few minutes later Rick says, "Downtown Carnage. Blink and you'll miss it."

We pass a bank, a couple of clothing stores, a beautifully main-tained old three story building with signs for a doctor, a dentist, an accountant, and a real estate agent out front. The movie theater boasts a marquee that has to be fifty years old, the kind where you place the letters by hand. There's an ice cream store, a pizza place. A wine bar. Some more shops. The whole of downtown extends maybe three or four blocks. I plan to hit every business here until I find a job.

Eventually the road dips down a gentle hill, and the buildings frame a narrow V of ocean. Then we round a corner and we're out of the main town, passing a couple of auto shops, a bowling alley, and some less than inviting squatty concrete buildings. And still we keep going. There are houses, but the distance between them grows wider and wider, the houses themselves set further and further back from the road.

Up ahead, where the coast juts into the ocean, a mansion sits at the edge of a cliff. We passed more than a few like it on the drive north, but this one feels different, isolated, cold, its lines stark and harsh. My skin tingles. My fingers and toes feel numb. I can't drag my gaze away from the house.

ComeComeComeComeComeHomeComeHomeComeHome...

Lightning flashes, turning the house into a silhouette. A long, low rumble of thunder follows.

The road curves. The view changes.

The house is no longer visible from the road.

I press my thumb and index finger against my closed lids. I feel woozy, lightheaded, like there are weights strapped to my temples and my neck is too weak to hold them. I hadn't realized I was this tired. It hit me like a kick to the head right after we left the Easy Mart.

When I open my eyes, it's to see a sign announcing that we're leaving Carnage Bay. I swivel to watch it disappear behind us as we keep going. My gut tightens, my nerves humming. "We just passed the sign that says we're leaving Carnage Bay. I thought my aunt lives in Carnage Bay."

Rick smiles at me, if pale lips drawn back to reveal tobacco-stained teeth can be called a smile. "Not exactly."

"Then where exactly does she live?" I'd been in Rick's truck for hours, since we left San Francisco. I'd felt uncomfortable with him since the second I met him, but now that discomfort swells like a sponge dropped in water.

It's raining again, water drumming on the roof with a steady beat, a thin stream breaching the faulty seal and snaking down the glass. But despite the weather and my exhaustion, I'm getting the feeling I'd be better off taking my chances out in the downpour than in the truck with Rick.

"I want to know exactly where we're going." My fingers curl around the door handle.

He makes a sound somewhere between a grunt and a laugh. "Don't get your panties in a wad, Lucian. It's just along here." He cuts a hard left onto what amounts to little more than a dirt path flanked by bushes and trees and unkempt grass as high as the tops of the tires.

My pulse kicks up and my palms go damp. We aren't on a main road anymore. We aren't anywhere near other cars or people.

I reach into the front pouch of my backpack and grab my key ring. Old keys. Useless keys, now. One is for the front door of the apartment building and one is for the back. One is for the storage locker. I don't know why I even kept them or why I brought them with. But at this moment, I'm glad I did. Keeping my hand down below my right thigh so Rick can't see, I form a fist with the longest key poking out beyond my curled baby finger. An improvised weapon.

Daph and I took a class in self-defense last year. They showed us how to go for the knee, the throat, the nose, the eyes, how to use a key ring or even a tightly rolled magazine as a weapon. Before that class, I thought the best way was to push all the keys between your fingers so they stuck out like spiky daggers. But the guy teaching the class said that would only work if you actually know how to throw a punch. I don't. So if Rick comes for me, I'll go for him with a hammer fist—the side of my fist and one protruding key—rather than my knuckles.

I focus on my breathing, trying to keep it slow and steady, trying not to telegraph my growing fear or my intent.

We round a bend and the trees break to an open lawn and a massive house standing against the backdrop of jagged whitecaps and raging ocean.

Rick slows to a stop. "*This* is exactly where your aunt lives," he says, making fun of my earlier demands that he tell me where we were going. "Ain't it pretty?"

Unease uncoils and stretches, coming alive in gradual degrees, climbing through me like a choking vine.

My gaze slides up the stone stairs, seeing them awash in stinging rain, feeling them hot beneath my bare feet under a blinding sun. Images and memories come at me, like I've been here before, lived here before.

Been afraid here before.

KISS ME GOODBYE—Coming Soon!

**Love futuristic action adventure romance?
Keep reading for a preview of *Driven*!**

SAMPLE CHAPTER FROM DRIVEN

The air was stale, rank with the stink of smoke, sweat, and old beer. Bob's Truck Stop. Nice place for a meal.

Raina Bowen sat at a small table, back to the wall, posture deceptively relaxed. Inside, she was coiled tighter than the Merckle shocks that were installed in her rig, but it was better to appear unruffled. Never let 'em see you sweat. That had been one of Sam's many mottos.

She glanced around the crowded room, mentally cataloguing the Siberian gun truckers at the counter, the cadaverous pimp in the corner and his ferret-faced companion, the harried waitress who deftly dodged the questing hand that reached out to snag her as she passed. In the center of the room was a small raised platform with a metal pole extending to the grime-darkened ceiling. A scantily clad girl—barely out of puberty—wiggled and twirled around the pole. Raina looked away. But for a single desperate act, one that had earned her freedom, she might have been that girl.

Idly spinning the same half-empty glass of warm beer that she'd been nursing for the past hour, she looked through the grimy windows at the front of the truck stop. Frozen, colorless, the bleak expanse stretched with endless monotony until the high-powered floodlights tapered off and the landscape was swallowed by the black night sky.

A balmy minus-thirty outside. And it would only get colder the farther north they went. Raina had a keen dislike of the cold, but if she were the first to reach Gladow Station with her load of genetically engineered grain, there'd be a fat bonus of fifty-million interdollars. That'd be more than enough to warm her to the cockles of her frozen heart.

More than enough to buy Beth's safety.

Keeping her gaze on the door, Raina willed it to open. She couldn't wait much longer. Where the hell was Wizard? Sitting here—a woman alone in a place like this—drew too much attention. She wanted no one to remember her face. Anonymity was a precious commodity, one she realized had slipped through her fingers as from the corner of her eye she watched one of the Siberians begin to weave drunkenly across the room.

"Well, hello, sweet thing." He stopped directly in front of her, kicked the extra chair out from the table, and shifted it closer before dropping his bulk onto the torn Naugahyde. He was shrouded in layers of tattered cloth that were stained and frayed, the stink of him hitting her nostrils before he finished his greeting.

"Leave. Now." Keeping her voice low and even, Raina snaked one hand along her waist toward the small of her back, resting her fingers on the smooth handle of her knife.

The Siberian smiled at her, revealing the brown stubs of three rotting teeth. "You can't chase me off so easy. I've been watching you." He gestured at the front of his pants. "You need a man, sweet thing."

Uh-huh. "And you think you're a man?"

The trucker frowned at her question. His thick brows shot up as he realized he'd been insulted. Undeterred, he leaned forward, catching her ponytail with one scarred and dirty hand. "I'll show you how much man I am. Give us a kiss, sweet thing."

His tongue was already out and reaching as he pulled her face closer to his.

"Last warning," Raina said softly, wishing he would listen.

He gave a hard tug on her ponytail. Raina slid her knife from its sheath, bringing it up with a sharp twist, neatly slicing through the tip of the trucker's tongue. Blood splattered in all directions, thick and hot. With an enraged howl he jerked back, letting loose his hold on her as he clapped both hands over his mouth. Dark blood dripped down his unshaven chin to pool on the tabletop.

Raina sent a quick look at the rest of the Siberians. Their attention was firmly fixed on the girl who was shimmying up and down the pole. Returning her gaze to the moaning trucker, she picked up the stained scrap of cloth that passed for a serviette and slowly wiped her blade clean. Serviettes used to be made of paper, but that was a long time ago, when there had still been enough trees to provide pulp.

She sighed. Anonymity was gone now. She'd have to settle for second best: adding to her reputation.

"Name's Raina Bowen," she said, "not sweet thing. And the last thing I need is a man."

Well, that wasn't exactly true. She needed one man in particular. Wizard. And she needed his precious trucking license. But he was nowhere to be seen.

The Siberian's eyes widened as he registered her name, and a flicker of recognition flared in their dull depths. Nice to have a reputation, even if she didn't quite deserve it. This lovely little encounter would just add to the mystique. Unfortunately, it would also add to the risk of being found. *Damn.*

He reached for her again, his hands rough, his expression stormy. He was mad, challenged, belittled, and he wanted revenge. What was it with Siberian gun truckers?

Twirling her hair around one finger, Raina shifted her expression, lowering her lashes over her blue eyes in a come-hither invitation, curving her lips in a winsome smile. The trucker blinked, clearly confused by her abrupt change in manner. He leaned in—Lord, some people never learned—and Raina deftly clipped him hard under the chin with the hilt of her knife.

He slumped across the Formica table, unconscious, mouth hanging open, leaving her with a blood splattered tabletop, a ruined beer, and an end to her patience.

His companions were looking this way now. Raina lowered her head as though enthralled by her table-mate, using her body to shield his inert form from view. Her ruse worked and the men nudged one another and laughed before turning back to the stripper.

Well, that had bought her about three minutes.

A sudden blast of light sliced through the frost-dusted window, spreading a glowing circle across the floor. Raina wondered if Wizard had finally arrived. Hope flared, and then faded. There was too much light for just one vehicle.

Trucks. Lots of 'em. They parked in a circle, the beams of their headlights illuminating a circumscribed area.

Like an arena.

She'd seen this set up before. The new arrivals were expecting entertainment—the kind that involved fists—and they were using their rigs to create the venue. She stared through the glass, the muscles of her shoulders and neck knotting with tension. Illegal gladiator games. There was going to be a bloodbath.

Hell. Wizard or not, she'd outstayed her time here. Tossing a handful of interdollars on the table, Raina shrugged into her parka and headed outside, staying well back in the shadows as she watched the scene unfold. The trucks were huge, as tall as two-storey houses, painted slate gray, and on the front in bold silver letters, the name JANSON.

Men were emerging from the cabs. Big, burly guys, dressed in hides and skins, bristling with weapons. Janson company men. How nice. The Janson owned the ICW—Intercontinental Worldwide—the longest highway ever built. Or at least, they acted like they did.

She could feel the tension in the air. Taste it. Someone had pissed these guys off, big-time.

At the far end of the lot was a lone truck. Nice transport. Black. Clean. Nameless. A non-company driver, just like her. Poor bastard. He was obviously tonight's planned entertainment.

"Hey, Big Luc," one of the Jansons yelled, moving into place in the circle that had formed. "That piece of crap jumped line. We gotta teach him some manners."

Jumped line? What moron would jump line on Janson trucks? They went first. It was an unwritten law. Anyone who flouted it was either insane or bent on a quick death. Raina watched as money exchanged hands. Odds were obviously in favor of Big Luc.

"Wizard's got some balls coming here tonight," a second man called. "He shoulda kept driving. Maybe we'd have let him live another day."

Wizard. Oh, no. Of all the morons in the frozen north, she had to hook up with the one who had picked a fight with a good portion of the Janson army. She narrowed her eyes at the huge black rig, the one at the far end of the lot. Wizard's rig. *Damn, damn, damn.*

He was of no use to her now. Still, she couldn't help but try to figure a way that she could salvage the trucking pass he was supposed to give her.

"Luc. Luc. Luc." The crowd was calling their champion.

In response to the cry, a huge man swaggered into the circle of light, raising his arms as he slowly spun around and around, egging on his admirers. Beneath the flat wool cap that clung to his skull, bushy brows drew down over a nose flattened and skewed to one side, and just below it bristled a thick thatch of mud-colored whiskers. An animal pelt hung over his massive shoulders, the head still intact, the jagged teeth catching the light.

Raina glanced again at the black rig at the far end of the lot. She'd never met Wizard, had contacted him on Sam's instructions—which in and of itself was a questionable recommendation—but she couldn't imagine he'd be any match for Luc. She had a hard time imagining *anyone* as a match for Luc.

The door of the cab opened, and a man swung down. He was tall, wearing a black parka, the hood pulled up, obscuring his features. She felt a moment's pity, and then squelched the unwelcome emotion. Not her fight. Not her business. Sam's words of loving fatherly advice rang in her head as clear as if he were standing beside her. *If there's no profit in it for you, stupid girl, then walk away. Just walk away. What do you care for some sucker's lousy luck?*

Not only was there no profit in it for her, but the jackass had cost her. Wizard was supposed to show up an hour ago with a temporary Janson trucking license that would allow her to jump the queue all nice and legal, behind the Janson but ahead of the other indies. Instead, he was an hour late, and he'd dragged a frigging army with him. Too bad the army wasn't on his side.

Wizard strode forward. He made it halfway across the parking lot, halfway to the door of the truck stop before Luc's fist connected with his face. Raina winced. She had a brief impression of long, dark hair as the hood fell back and Wizard's head snapped sideways. He went down, rolling head over heels across the inflexible sheet of solid ice.

In three strides Luc was on him, the steel reinforced toe of his company-issue boots finding a nice home right between Wizard's ribs. Wizard didn't move, didn't moan, and for a second Raina wondered if that first punch had knocked him out cold. With a laugh, Luc kicked him again, and then nudged him with his boot, once, twice. He backed off, waving at the group that surrounded him, shaking hands as he slowly made his way toward the door of the diner, acting as though he'd just rid the world of public enemy number one.

The remaining Jansons closed in, a pack of avid rats, eyes glittering with malevolent intent. There was no doubt in Raina's mind that they were going to beat Wizard within an inch of his life, a warning to anyone who tried to cross them.

Raina glanced at her snowscooter. She'd been smart enough to park her rig in a safe place and use the scooter to get her to the truck stop. No sense inviting trouble. Now she wondered if she could maneuver into the circle of men surrounding Wizard's prone form, nab him, and get them both out of here before someone got killed. She hesitated, the thought going against her instinct for self-preservation. Why she was even considering this she couldn't say. Hadn't Sam Bowen beaten all compassion out of her? *Stupid girl. Empathy will only get you killed.*

Squelching the voice in her head, she focused on the guy sprawled across the frozen ground. He had the damned trucking license, and she needed it. All she had to do was figure a way to get it.

She cringed as Wizard pushed himself to his feet. Shaking his head as if to clear it, he wiped the back of his hand across his mouth. God, he didn't even have the sense to stay down.

"Hey, Luc," he called softly, the sound of his voice drawing Raina up short. Low, rich, a sensual baritone that sent a shiver up her spine.

"While you're in there, you want to fetch me a beer?" He immitated Luc's drawl to perfection.

Raina closed her eyes and sighed. Dim. Thick. Brainless. He was a dead man. And all for the sake of what? His machismo? She shifted, trying to get a look at his face, but he'd pulled his hood up again.

Big Luc turned slowly to face him. "You got a death wish, boy?"

"Name's Wizard, and the only thing I'm wishing for is a long cold beer." Oh, that slow, lazy drawl. It should be illegal for a guy that dumb to have a voice that smooth.

"Well, Wiiiiz-aaard..." Luc guffawed, slapping one fleshy palm on his thigh. "You ready to die?"

Run. Run. Run. You might have a chance. Raina willed him to move. Big Luc would kill him and leave his frozen carcass in the snow. The wild dogs would pick him clean, and no one would care. She'd make herself not care.

Luc lunged at him. Raina expected Wizard to step back, to dodge, to move. Instead, he shot out one fist with lightning speed, and dropped Luc in his tracks.

She blinked, certain her brain was processing something other than what her eyes had seen.

For a moment she waited, convinced that Luc would get up, would charge like an enraged bull and cut Wizard down. Without a backward look, Wizard turned and strode in the direction of the diner, as if he hadn't just accomplished the impossible. As if he hadn't just invited his own assassination.

And, oh, the *way* he moved... confident, fluid, a man comfortable in his own skin. Raina watched him for a long moment, and then looked away, wondering what the hell was wrong with her. Why should she care about the easy way some useless gun trucker moved his hips?

Whoooo. Get it together, Bowen.

No one spoke. No one moved. It felt like no one dared breathe, and then two guys stepped forward, hauled Big Luc up by his armpits, and dragged him away.

Stupid man. Stupid, stupid man. Wizard had just made a mighty powerful enemy in the Janson Trucking Company. Actually, they'd been his enemies from the second he'd jumped line, but they might have let him live... suffer, but live. Maybe. Now she didn't think so. They were likely to gut him and feed his intestines down his own throat.

Her breath hissed from between her teeth. She needed the Gladow winnings. For herself. For Beth.

She *needed* that temporary license, which meant she was just as stupid as Wizard was, because she was about to step into his fight.

Hugging the shadows, she sprinted to the edge of the wall, climbed onto her snowscooter, and gunned the engine. She spun the scooter in an arc. Heart racing, she stopped sharply near the door of the truck stop, just behind the dumb jackass who had so thoroughly messed up her plans.

"Get on," Raina shouted. Several of the Janson men were closing in, and she was glad that the hood of her anorak hid her features from view. She could only pray that they wouldn't recognize her. *Yeah, right.* And if by some miracle they didn't, all they had to do was ask around at Bob's and the Siberian she'd cut would be only too happy to provide her name. This was her night for dumb choices. "If you have one iota of sense, *get on*."

Wizard whipped around to face her. For a frozen moment he stood silhouetted against the light streaming from the window behind him. She thought he would prove that he lacked even that one iota of sense she'd mentioned, for he just stood there, his head tilted as he watched the line of Janson truckers who were slowly stalking him, closing in behind her. She could sense them, see the hazy reflections of their faces in the windows of the truck stop at Wizard's back.

Then with a shrug, he swung one long leg over the seat of the snowscooter, his arms coming around her waist as he climbed on.

Raina gunned the engine and took off into the star-tossed night. Heart racing, she set the speed as fast as she dared, knowing the dangers of hitting a deep rut at high speed. Knowing, too, that there was a strong likelihood they'd be followed. Even over the noise of the engine she could hear the roar of a mob denied.

Heat exploded in a shimmering wave, and for an instant, night turned to day as someone fired a round of plas-shot.

Wizard's reaction had to be instinctive. He pushed up tight against her back, protecting her with his body. With a hiss, she jerked her elbow sharply into his gut, sending the message that she didn't need him to act like human armor. *Moron.*

She could feel him behind her, pressed up against her back, his muscled thighs melded to hers, his arms forming a solid vise around her waist. He was bigger than she had expected. When he'd stepped down from his truck, all she'd registered was the size of Big Luc, the danger posed by the Janson drivers.

She'd thought Wizard their harmless prey.

Now, with the feel of his long, hard body pushed up against her, she wondered how she could have been so wrong.

She shifted forward a couple of inches, putting as much space between them as she could. Her thoughts turned back to the men they'd left behind. She knew for certain that the Janson hadn't expected anyone to play savior to their chosen quarry. And since she'd been fool enough to take on the role... well, she could only hope that she'd not been recognized, and that the Siberian was too embarrassed to admit he'd been cut by a woman. Making an enemy of Janson Trucking was fool's work. And that fool was on the back of her snowscooter.

Annoyance curled through her. Now that she'd saved him, just where was she supposed to take him? She stared out into the night, endless star-stippled sky above a frozen waste. *His* rig was parked back at the truck stop, and until the Janson left, she'd be wiser not to return there. *Her* rig was parked to the east, on a little-known access road that actually led to nowhere—a throwback to the days before the Fossil Fuel Edict of 2089. She turned east, mentally chastising herself for getting involved in something that was none of her affair. But, hell, she needed that license because she *was* going to win that race to Gladow Station.

The bite of the wind had grown bitter, and Raina tugged her hood closer around her face as she drove. Some thirty minutes passed before the outline of her truck loomed ahead, a bulky, dark silhouette against the midnight sky, chrome trim highlighted by the beam of the snowscooter's headlight.

"Home, sweet home," she muttered as she killed the engine and climbed off the seat, pulling the hood of her parka back. The frigid air slapped her skin as she stalked forward, and she was glad for the discomfort. Maybe it would smack some sense into her. Lord knew she'd left hers in the lot outside the truck stop when she'd offered a ride to Wizard.

Expecting him to be right behind her, she keyed in the code, opened the door of the cab, and climbed inside. She spoke over her shoulder as she flicked on the light. "You can lie low here for the night, get your truck tomorrow. Big Luc and his friends will either be gone by morning, or too drunk to notice when you come back for your rig. Either way, you aren't going anywhere tonight. Too dangerous."

When there was no reply, Raina turned and found to her exasperation that Wizard was leaning against the snowscooter, arms crossed, long legs outstretched, face obscured by the hood of his anorak. He was no more than a dark shadow on an equally dark night. His posture was comfortable, relaxed, as though the glacial chill was no more than a temperate breeze.

"Are you planning to sleep out there?" she called.

"Preferably not." He rose and crossed the space that separated them. The light from the cab leaked across the snow, then across him as he stepped into the circle of its scattered rays. "But it is impolite to enter another's domicile without an invitation."

The cadence of his words, his tone, they sounded different now that he wasn't mimicking Luc.

"You want an invitation to my domicile?" She snorted. "Won't you join me for tea?" *Moron.*

Raina had a fleeting impression of dark hair spilling from beneath his hood before he ducked his head and climbed up the side of the cab. She stepped back to let him in, unfastened the catch-seam of her own parka and hung it on the hook behind the driver's seat.

She led the way into the small living quarters that backed off the driver's cabin. She felt awkward having him here. Gesturing to the plasma screen set into one wall of her rig, she spoke over her shoulder, babbling as she tried to cover her discomfort. "I can track six satellites, and over four thousand channels. Used to be seven satellites, but I think an orbit decayed."

Her companion made no reply. It appeared that he wasn't interested in small talk. Fine by her. She wasn't particularly adept at it herself.

She snatched a pile of microdisks off the plastitech chair, clutched them against her chest, and looked around for somewhere to put them. The chair was the only place to sit other than the bed, and she wasn't about to offer him *that*. Hazarding a glance over her shoulder, Raina checked just to make certain he was still there. Her breath skidded to a stunned stop.

He was right behind her, his tall frame a hand span away. Up close, with his hood thrown back, the catch-seam of his parka undone, Wizard didn't look helpless at all. A day's growth of beard shaded the chiseled plane of his jaw, and his full lips were drawn into a hard line. He looked dangerous, self-assured, frightening. Not a man who'd needed saving.

Hugging the microdisks like a shield, Raina tipped her head back and met his eyes. Slate gray. Cold. She swallowed. What the hell had she been thinking to bring him here? He wasn't some lost puppy who needed a warm place to sleep.

Get Driven now!

~

COMPACT OF SORCERERS SERIES

Demon's Kiss (Book 1)

Demon's Hunger (Book 2)

Trinity Blue (short story)

~

THE GAME SERIES (YOUNG ADULT)

Rush (Book 1)

Push (Book 2)

Crash (Book 3)

Join Eve's Reader Group for the latest info about contests, new releases and more! www.EveSilver.net

ABOUT THE AUTHOR

(photo credit: Shanon Fujioka)

National bestselling author Eve Silver has been praised for her "edgy, steamy, action-packed" books, darkly sexy heroes and take-charge heroines. In 2015 she won the OLA Forest of Reading White Pine Award, her work was shortlisted for the Monica Hughes Award for Science Fiction and Fantasy (2014), and was both an American Bookseller's Association Best Book for Children and a Canadian Children's Book Centre Best Books for Kids and Teens (2013). She has garnered starred reviews from *Publishers Weekly*, *Library Journal*, and *Quill and Quire*, two *RT Book Reviews* Reviewers' Choice Awards, *Library Journal's* Best Genre Fiction Award, and she was nominated for the Romance Writers of America® RITA® Award. Eve lives with her husband, two sons, an energetic Airedale terrier and an exuberant border collie/shepherd. And a snake called Ragnar.

Join Eve's Reader Group for the latest info about contests, new releases and more!

Find Eve online at

www.evesilver.net

Made in United States
Troutdale, OR
01/23/2024

17078451R00126